NOW SHOWING

MASCULINITY: TOXIC

Staff/Contributing Writers:

Lucienne LeBeau
S.N. Humphreys
Sarah E. Blackburn

Staff/Contributing Artists:

Michael Strong
Nix Black

Associate Editor: Lucienne LeBeau

Managing Editor: w.p. Quigley

An Ascendent Publishing Title
All Rights Reserved®
Winter 2023 Issue #2

DOUBLE FEATURE

TABLE OF CONTENTS:

Welcome to the Theatre

We've got nonpareils, soda and all of the popcorns!
But pay no attention to the usher with the black horns
He'll give you a spot to sit in a comfy seat
Bring your sweater—as they turn down the heat.

Turn those phones off and keep your voice down
Or that usher with horns will give you a frown.
You might find yourself in a bit of a snit
As he tosses you out and calls you a tit.

You're here to see mayhem and tales full of madness
So sip your beverage and watch with gladness.
Two stories of masculinity toxic unfold
And micro tales for those who are bold.

Lucienne LeBeau spins a tale filled with dread
Of rapists and vengeance and a quick severed head.
With a following tale of murder and ripping
Keep turning the page—to the end—NO SKIPPING.

You'll want to see how it all turns out
With tales from Humphreys and Strong no doubt.
Take a break with the poet called Blackburn, she's divine
And yes we allow you to bring your own wine.

A cover so clever by Michael Strong
And art by Nix Black—you just can't go wrong.
Then writers will step back in with their magic
So hold on tight, as the endings are tragic

You paid your admission, and here is your ticket
Outside are the protestors making their picket
But you dared to enter, and so you will play
Where all of the demons entice you to stay.

The lights are dim, and the curtains arise
As your heart beats a rhythm of certain demise.
Fear not what lies in the room—dark and doubt
But take Lucienne's hand, for she knows the way out.

-Lucienne LeBeau
December 24, 2022

HAVE THE DAY YOU DESERVE

by S.N Humphreys

Mortimer Heep sat hunched over the counter at Atomic Comics, sucking down a reuben as three young women entered the shop. Bimbos, he thought, as he wiped sauerkraut from the corner of his mouth. What the hell do they want?

Mort was of medium height and weighed about the same as a wet paper bag. His hair was a dull, slightly greasy brown. His eyes were small and squinty, his nose just a tad large, and more than a little crooked.

He had nothing much in the way of friends or family, and outside of his job at Atomic Comics, few interests. He'd started work stocking the shelves as a teenager. Now thirty-two, Atomic Comics was his own little kingdom.

That suited Mort just fine. He could read comics all day, order what he liked, and get paid to do so. He had hoped to become a writer or artist, but teachers and critics ensured he knew that he lacked both the creativity and the talent. He was built to consume, not create. Some people might be discouraged by such criticisms, but not Mort. He was a realist.

The three girls wandered the shop, perusing the shelves as Mort turned his attention back to them. He took in their dyed hair, heavy makeup, and torn up clothes. Emos, he decided.
He snorted. Emo poseurs. His semi-erection annoyed him, and he adjusted his seat. Would definitely give it to the one with no tits.

The girls whispered to each other, shooting furtive glances at him. Mort rolled his eyes and heaved a loud, heavy sigh. The girls approached the counter, the middle one clearing her throat as the other two hung slightly behind.

"Excuse me, sorry, have you got any copies of 'Dinner Witch' in?"

Dinner Witch? These dumb bitches were looking for Dinner Witch?

"That's a kid's book," Mort informed them.

The three girls exchanged a look.

"I mean, sure, but we like it," said the chubby one.

Mort stared at them for a few seconds, then bellowed with laughter.

"Look, have you got it or not?"

The titless one is losing her temper, thought Mort, hot.

"Yeah, sure. You want to read garbage, we keep it in the boxes towards the back. Listed alphabetically." Mortimer gave a lazy wave towards the back of the shop.

The girls went to look for their comic, the smaller one who'd succeeded in giving Mort a raging boner by this point shot him a look of pure loathing as her friends pulled her towards the back.

"Fucking dumb poseur bitches," Mortimer mumbled. Oh great, here comes the fat one. And she's got a stack of those stupid kid stories.

"We'll take these."

3

This girl, this girl with her shitty comics and her pink hair, her fishnets and black lipstick, THIS GIRL was looking directly over his shoulder, avoiding eye contact like he was a steaming pile of shit.

"That'll be twenty-four ninety-five and the last shreds of your dignity." Mortimer Heep smirked at the sudden stiffening of the girl's entire body, knowing he'd gotten to her.

"Here you go," she said, dropping her cash on the counter and grabbing the books. "Keep the change, I don't want it."

The other two girls were murmuring something unintelligible. The girl with the books joined them. They clasped hands and the middle one, the skinny red haired one looked Mort dead in the eye. There was a sudden rushing in his ears, like water filling up a bucket. Something about that look caused an outbreak of chills all over his body. Fear lodged in his chest. He shivered and looked away with haste.

The red head spat on the floor, and the three girls stalked out of the shop, laughing.

Mortimer Heep closed up shop, all the while scratching at his burning crotch. It had started slowly, not long after those emo bitches left the shop, and had built up to a serious forest fire in his pants. He'd have thought it was an STD, if he wasn't fully aware that no one but him had ever handled his cock.

Those mentally deficient dick teases had given him a raging boner, and now his junk was on fire. Worse than fucking useless. Mort walked towards his bus stop a bit like a cowboy in one of those old western films, with his legs bowed to avoid inflaming his manhood any further. It wasn't helping.

The 32 showed up right on time, and Mort sat in the first seat. They were meant for the old and disabled, but he didn't care. Why should he? No one was in them anyway. He spread his legs out to take up both seats and let his head loll back.

It was two stops later when he heard a throat clearing and felt a gentle tug on his shirt. His eyes snapped open to see an old woman. She was at least 70, and lucky if she was 5 feet tall. She had a small basket on wheels. She smiled at him.

"Excuse me, young man, I was wondering if..."

"Oh bore off! The whole bus is empty, take any other seat. I'm not moving. Fucking old biddy."

The old woman tutted at him and hobbled off to the next row, struggling to get her trolley to fit down the aisle. Mortimer Heep scratched his arm.

"What the fuck is this world coming to," he muttered, "I work hard! I'm a contributing member of society. How dare that old bitch expect me to move? Her fucking legs seem to work fine to me."

When the bus finally pulled up to his stop, there was a woman waiting with two small, snot-nosed children. She had an air of exhaustion and her children looked bored and dim. They attempted to bundle onto the bus as soon as the door opened. She pulled them back.

"Let the nice man off first," the woman instructed them. "Sorry about that." She looked up at Mort whose face was starting to sprout what appeared to be boils and flinched at the sight of him.

"Yes, you certainly are," he spat out, rolling his eyes and pushing past the children. He walked towards his building mumbling, "Stupid slut should have tried using some birth control." He felt like he was burning up from the inside. What fresh hell was this? He couldn't afford to get the flu now, he had rent coming due next week.

As Mort rounded the corner, he spied a young homeless runaway standing outside his building. She was chatting with a few of the usual bums, who cleared off as Mort drew closer.

"Oh, for fuck's sake, not this shit," he mumbled, looking at his reflection in a car window. The face staring back at him was covered in sores. There was an audible pop as one exploded and leaked pus down his pock-marked cheek.

Mort tried to remember if he'd ever had chickenpox before.

"Hey man, you got some spare change?" The girl's gaze darted about, only landing on him briefly. Her cropped black hair was dirty, as were the many layers of clothes she was bundled in.

"Listen you fucking freeloader, your whore of a mother should be supporting you. Go home or get a fucking job!"

Mort's head was pounding like one of those shitty hippie drum circles. HIs vision was going blurry. He stumbled up the steps and through the door. "Here I am, working myself to death, and this stupid fucking kid is too dumb to stay at home where everything is free."

The elevator was empty, thankfully. Mort closed his eyes, not noticing the pus and blood dripping from his face. He was distracted by his weak, hot, and heavy arms. When he finally looked down at them, they seemed to swim in his vision–a kaleidoscope of skin and hair dancing before his eyes. He ham-fisted the button for the third floor.

Mort swayed in the lift, vision swimming and dimming. He wondered if he would faint before he got inside his flat. The elevator stopped and the door opened with a ding onto the 3rd floor. Mort stumbled out, too sick to realize he was leaving a wet, sticky trail behind him like some sort of demented slug-man.

The hallway smelled of someone cooking a delicious curry dinner.

"ARE YOU FUCKING KIDDING ME?" Mortimer Heep gargled out the words. His throat seemed to be filled with phlegm. The widowed Indian woman who lived next door to him opened her door to see what was going on, then slammed it shut in fear. He could hear the locks being latched. "Do you fucking people ever eat anything besides goddamned curry? I'm so sick... of the smell... of fucking... curr–"

It was at this point that Mort's vision went black.

His eye sockets felt as if they overflowed with molten lava. Mort's eyeballs spontaneously liquified, running down his sagging, blistered countenance.

He reached out his arms towards his apartment door and stumbled, gargling out a gasp at the anticipation of the cold hard ground when he hit it. There was no cold hard ground to hit as the heat intensified. Body popping and gurgling, he dissolved into a massive puddle of pus and blood and bubbling flesh.

His welcome mat sizzled in the toxic mess of what was once the meat of Mortimer Heep.

GIRL
FALLOUT
SHELTER
5 MI

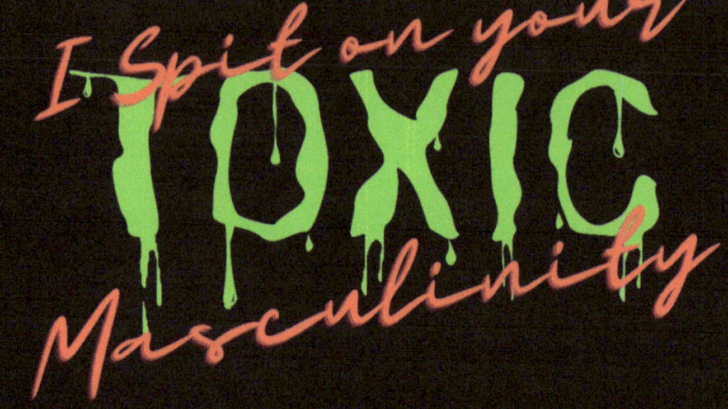

RAPE, SEXPLOITATION, AND RAPE REVENGE GRINDHOUSE FILMS

By Haarlotte O'Scara

Sex is supposed to be a fun activity between two or more consenting adults. Whether it's a gangbang on a rainy afternoon in your orgy pit, surrounded by condoms and snacks (you gotta have snacks, come on), or a hot and heavy date for two, ideally it should be a great time had by all.

Rape is the disgusting antithesis to sex.

It is the removal of bodily autonomy of the victim, and an act of violence and exertion of power over the person being raped. It can be perpetuated by any gender against any gender. For those who have gone through it, it is the worst thing that has ever happened to them, and they are not able to forget it.

It is, in and of itself, horror. Reality for far too many in these United States.

According to the Rape, Abuse & Incest National Network (RAINN) found at rainn.org, "1 out of every 6 American women has been the victim of an attempted or completed rape in her lifetime (14.8% completed, 2.8% attempted). About 3% of American men—or 1 in 33—have experienced an attempted or completed rape in their lifetime."

If you're uncomfy with where this is going, good. Sit with the uncomfortable thought that out of every six women you know, the possibility of one of them having been the victim of rape or attempted rape is their reality, and 1 out of 33 men have been, too.

And those are just the ones who reported.
We can't know how many decided not to share their experiences.

Rape is the enemy of sex.

It takes a good time between consenting adults and sullies it, leaving its victims in a personal hell where they themselves feel defiled. If they choose to share what happened, in come the badgering questions from the "it'll never happen to me" crowd.

What were you wearing? Where were you? What were you thinking going into that alley? Why did you take that shortcut? What were you doing at that party anyway? Why did you take that drink from them? Why didn't you call someone? Why did you stay? Why did you leave early? What did you think they were going to do?

Both men and women ask questions like this from the victim/survivor, essentially making them relive the rape over and over again as if they weren't doing that already.

Rape can happen anywhere, and does: in prisons, at schools, at churches, and even in the discomfort of your own home. There are different types of rape: corrective rape (where a rapist decides he or she can fuck a person into being straight), date rape, prison rape, etc. It's ubiquitous and conspicuous, and yet, our culture tries to pretend it's not all that big a deal.

I know, this is a heavy, gross subject. I wish it were about popcorn's history in the theater like W.P. Quigley's was. But I'm the projectionist this time around and Mama O'Scara's gotta tell you all about the heavy stuff before we can delve into the history of rape revenge in cinema.

Ah, there we go. Two words that go together almost like peanut butter and jelly: rape revenge.

Many victims/survivors of rape delve into anger fantasies (anger is a natural phase of grief, and rape causes a great deal of grief in a person's life) of cutting the dicks off their perpetrators, sewing their hands to their vulvae, or otherwise causing them as much pain as they sustained when they were violated. Some dream of hunting down their assailant and butchering them. Still others want to flat out shoot their rapists in the head.

So many would just like to forget. Once the anger phase passes, the need for revenge does, too. Sometimes.

Other times it lingers.

All of this is 'normal' and expected.

While rape and revenge films have been around quite a bit longer, they were handled differently throughout the history of film. For example, Diary of a Lost Girl (1929, starring the ethereal Louise Brooks) has the main character, Thymian, raped by the druggist, then later gets pregnant, gets sent to a reformatory school, runs away, and works at a brothel. After that commentary on how women who are raped become "whores," we see an upswing in revenge films where the father is the protector of a young woman's "purity."

Alfred Hitchcock Presents: Revenge (originally aired October 2, 1955) is a television broadcast, however, the filmmaker made it and it is considered a gold standard of this particular theme.

Side note: they were not allowed to say "rape" on television, so they substituted "killed" instead.

Anyway, this cemented the idea that it was up to fathers to protect their daughters and seek revenge on the rapist themselves.

Enter Ingmar Bergman and his film The Virgin Spring, a 1960 film where a father seeks revenge for the rape of his daughter.

It wasn't until 1970 that we began to see a steady rise in the empowerment of women enacting their own revenge.

Well, sort of.

Let's kick off with Wes Craven's Last House on the Left (1972). A version of Virgin Spring, but MORE (because, Americans like MORE). Let's have lots of rapes in this film and big revenge enacted by dear old Dad.

Interestingly enough (I'll get to this later), Roger Ebert praised this film as being "a tough, bitter little sleeper of a movie that's about four times as good as you'd expect." I did not expect Ebert to enjoy it as much as he did, so it seems that Last House hit the mark as a quintessential rape revenge film.

During the 1970s, my pretties, women were making serious progress in the arena of civil rights. With the advent of the pill (birth control, my fiends, birth control), women were taking control of their bodies and enjoying the fuck out of fucking.

There was empowerment there, but there was a patriarchy to fight. White women had more freedom and mobility than women of color (and we're still feeling and reeling from this today), and often silenced women of color and their issues while focusing on their own. Many of these movies, as a result, focus on the experience of the white woman.

Through the male gaze.

What's the male gaze, you didn't ask? You had no intention of asking? Well, then, you already know what it is—that it's the theory from Laura Mulvey that the male gaze is the scopophilic engagement with the enjoyment of looking at women in the same way one looks at an object. Good. Very good.

Now I don't have to tell you to try to keep up. You've got this, champ.

I'm just kidding. But did you feel like you were being condescended, even for a second? That's how a lot of women felt and feel to this day, living under the scrutiny of men and other women, trying to fit into an ideal that doesn't actually exist. This happens to men, too. And it happened in droves in the 1970s, particularly to women.

That, and rape was becoming something that people really talked about, not just alluded to, and rape revenge films became an answer to that.

Now, before I delve into this, I have to say—this is about discussing rape in the lens of fiction. The harsh reality is even grittier. No one ever deserves to be raped, and no one should ever have to go through it. Ever.

Dealing with a heavy subject like this can help people cope. Remember, fiction is a safe space where the reader or viewer can turn away, back into the comfort of their home or theater, among people who are their safety.

So in the interest of space, I'm not going to expand on how many rape revenge films are out there—there are plenty and if you're interested, seek them out—I'm just going to focus on one.

The one that is considered a grindhouse standard yet is relatively unknown among today's audiences (and no, it's not Last House on the Left from 1972, though that one is pure genius from Wes Craven, may he rest in pieces): it's I SPIT ON YOUR GRAVE.

My autocomplete doesn't know it at all—it keeps trying to correct it to "I spit on your gravy" which would make a great Thanksgiving revenge film come to think of it—and that's saying something. I Spit On Your Grave (1978) was remade/rebooted in 2010, but the remake had nowhere near the teeth of 1978.

The one from 1978? If you are sensitive, don't watch it. It's very raw. Visceral, and exploitative. The rape scene from 2010 has nowhere near the gruesome brutality that the 1978 rape scene has. It is a gang rape where four men torture a young writer who is staying alone in a cabin in the woods. The setting is idyllic, the rape is profane.

It makes her revenge all the more satisfying.

It follows the three-act formula that's seen in typical rape revenge films.

Act One: Victim is raped.
Act Two: Victim survives and recovers.
Act Three: Now a survivor, the clear-headed person enacts their revenge on the perpetrator(s).

This is typically a woman as the main character/victim, gathering her power and seeking revenge on those who did her harm.

Being set in 1978, ISOYG was a grindhouse favorite, and played in 1980 at even prestigious theaters in Chicago (Plitt's United Artists, according to Roger Ebert, much to his chagrin). Ebert hated the film, by the way, no less for the audience's reaction to it. It sickened him. (He was a pretty gentle soul from what I've heard, bless him.)

He missed the point. Then again, I don't think there was much of a point to the film except for pure exploitative violent symmetry. The violence of rape, followed by the violence of murder and maiming.

But for grindhouse fans, the film was well received. Unsurprisingly, some men in the audience enjoyed the rape scenes as they were presented as highly charged sexually (and with the lens of male gaze), and some women enjoyed the revenge scenes (see Roger Ebert's review from July 16, 1980).

My reaction, through my born in 1975 lens of an aging and bitter Gen-Xer? I hate that audience with a passion (okay more like apathy), but I appreciate the film for what it was: an attempt to give symmetry to violence and a way to give a victim a voice.

And that's all there is on the surface. We could take a deeper dive into the implications of living in rape culture where jokes about it abound, and when those jokes are "okay," if ever. Briefly. I don't have much space here to expand on the subject.

Lens and context. We will always come back to the lens—who is doing the viewing—and context—what the surrounding circumstances are. A survivor telling a rape joke hits differently than a perpetrator telling it. The survivor doing the telling is trying to use humor as a defense. A perpetrator telling it is disgusting and making an attempt to punch down. Again. The audience laughing is a different story as well. Some laugh when they're uncomfortable. Some laugh because they think it's genuinely funny, and some laugh to keep from screaming.

It is similar for a rape revenge film. While the filmmaker is not responsible for how an audience reacts (and may be horrified by their reactions), they are 100% responsible for the content they create and their intentions.

The rape scenes must, for a revenge film to be successful, be so brutal that the viewer despises the antagonist(s). So much so that the protagonist's technicolor violent revenge is equal to the brutality they suffered.

There is also a twofold message to women in 1978 in this film: one, do not travel alone and two, do not assert yourself. You will be punished in the most spectacular fashion.

In addition to that, you will have to seek justice/revenge all on your own.

There is no one to help you, believe you, or support you. Therefore, you must do it yourself. DIY justice. DIY revenge.

Maybe today we could and would do them differently—and maybe we could get people talking about dismantling rape culture. I don't want to go back. I don't want to deal with audiences cheering on a rape.

I don't want a world where rape is acceptable violence. It would be so much better to have a world where this was considered antiquated fiction. But that's not going to happen, and pretending it doesn't exist isn't going to make it go away.

Maybe today's rape revenge films could be done differently, where they could tell a story of the victim finding their voice, playing off of ISOYG to really examining the lives of the independent human. But then it wouldn't be the grotesquerie hyperviolence that the grindhouse niche audience enjoys.

I haven't seen ISOYG Deja Vu, but it is on my Tubi list (as of this writing I haven't seen it, but that will likely change by the time this is printed). I'm wondering, following Jennifer Hills (played by the wonderful Camille Keaton as she reprises her role), what shape this film will take. What will 40 years later be like for the victim who got her revenge?

Looking forward to seeing what's changed, what's remained the same, and what we still need to work on.

In reality, remember: She's more than just somebody's daughter. He's more than somebody's son. They're more than that. They're people—people who exist for their own purposes, and the revenge should come from a place where this person, objectified, says 'no more' and exacts their pound of flesh.

John Bloom (aka Joe Bob Briggs), is an obvious fan of the film and I am in his camp. This visceral tale not only hits all the marks for peak grindhouse, it gives some of us an outlet for our anger phase at what was done or almost done to us, beyond our control.

Remember, fictional tellings are our safety in a world that presents us with the unsafe. For many people, this is a refuge where we can explore the base and vile, and then come out of it clean.

Some do not want to relive it, and that's okay. But some of us need it. It's part of our therapy.

But that's another subject for another time.

Make no mistake: men, women, and non-binary people are all negatively affected by toxic masculinity. As you read through the shorts and the features, remember that victims come in all shapes and sizes, and the survivor in fiction (much like real life) doesn't always get revenge.

That's why, in real life, a focus on justice is the way to go.

Oh, and one more thing before I show the features for your reading/viewing pleasure—if you are sensitive to this subject and it hurts to read, put it down and walk away. This issue is not for you, and you may not be in a place where this entertains you. You may also find it cathartic, however, but ultimately the choice to read this is yours and yours alone.

The reality of rape is a horror that far too many people have to live with. RAINN, the Rape, Abuse & Incest National Network is a transparent, nonprofit organization in the US dedicated to education, prevention, and assistance for those who have been victimized. I hope you'll consider dropping them a few bucks if you can spare it. Because as much as we love a good revenge story, we can always return to our safe spaces. Survivors can't always do that.

From their mission statement:

RAINN (Rape, Abuse & Incest National Network) is the nation's largest anti-sexual violence organization. RAINN created and operates the National Sexual Assault Hotline (800.656.HOPE, online.rainn.org y rainn.org/es) in partnership with more than 1,000 local sexual assault service providers across the country and operates the DoD Safe Helpline for the Department of Defense. RAINN also carries out programs to prevent sexual violence, help survivors, and ensure that perpetrators are brought to justice.

Together we can carve out spaces for survivors to just breathe.

LIPSTICK Atomic

CRUMMIE

Dizzy didn't like it when Crummie came home early from Lipstick Atomic. He always stank of booze and his usual B.O. And he always looked at her wrong. Especially if he didn't have enough credits to buy a friend for the night.

Dizzy didn't go near that place. The sex workers were okay, she guessed, but all that kind of stuff made her uncomfy. Mostly she just liked to grow her vegetables, biggest veggies for sale in all of New Crescent City thanks much—and trade for coffee beans at the Haggle Huts. Her most recent obsession in her whole life (all 20 years of it) was growing coffee in the sour soil.

She had a knack for growing things, Crummie said with that lecherous look on his face. Dizzy always blushed and looked away. If she looked too long he might think she was interested.

Gross.

The sunset was almost here, and Dizzy finished weeding, pulling the edible grasses into one basket, and compost into the other. She would make salad, save aside a plate for Crummie, and hopefully he wouldn't be around to eat it till tomorrow.

When she heard the footsteps behind her, her shoulders slumped.

"You spend a lot of time on your knees," Crummie said, his words slurred. She could smell the hooch and rancid odor of his sweat.

Dizzy finished her weeding and dumped the compost bucket out. She wouldn't look at him.

He burped and scratched at his crotch. "Hey—I said, you spend a lot of time on your knees."

Dizzy gripped her edible grass basket and looked down at her feet. "I heard you the first time. Do you want dinner?"

"No. I want to get laid," he said.

"You should go back to Lipstick." Dizzy said, scurrying past him.

He reached out and grabbed her, his fat hand encircling the circumference of her upper arm. "Why should I? They ran fresh outta whores and I don't do the guy whores."

Dizzy looked up at him. She didn't want to shake under his grip, but she did.

"Please let me go so I can make dinner. We got good meat and I don't want to waste it," she said, instantly regretting her choice of words.

"I got good meat, too. Maybe tonight's the night, Dizz."

She swallowed hard and wriggled out of his grip. "Come on, be serious, Crummie. That's gross."

As she darted into the house, she heard him laugh.

Dizzy made a decent meal—roasted potatoes fresh from the garden, a grass and green salad, and roasted curry goat. Crummie didn't eat any of it, instead swigging from his moonshine jug and burping out songs that were old when their grandparents were born. Dizzy had learned to tune it out.

She had cleaned her plate and was about to get up and clear the table when he slammed the jug down on it, rattling the cutlery and making her jump out of her chair. Crummie laughed.

"You stupid bitch, where's my plate?" Crummie asked.

"You said you didn't want any," Dizzy said.

She shook as she stood and grabbed the plate. Maybe if she moved fast, he wouldn't catch her.

He mocked her shaking and repeated back to her in a high-pitched whine, " you said you didn't want any, meh-meh-meh-meh-meh-meh-meh." Crummie looked up at her. " Well I change-ed up my mind."

"Well, go ahead and serve yourself a plate," Dizzy said. " I'm really tired from working all day."

Crummie stood up and knocked the table on its side, grabbing Dizzy by both her arms. Plate and cutlery clattered to the floor and she yelped.

"I didn't nearly die trying to save Momma and Daddy just to get treated like this, you stupid cunt. No, I'm not taking nothing off you."

His warm mouth, slimy and dripping, pressed against hers. He flicked his tongue in her mouth. Dizzy gagged and pulled away. Crummie held her fast.

Oh, no. You're not one of them whores. You can't throw me outta my own home, you little bitch. No, tonight's my night. I'm getting my way this time."

Dizzy screamed, but to Crummie, it sounded like a squeal of delight. The more she tried to wrest herself from his grip, the tighter he held her.

He ripped her shirt off and clawed at her. She stepped away, bare foot slamming down on the fork that had dropped not moments before. This time, she howled.

"Oh yeah! This is gonna be fun!" Crummie undid his pants and threw Dizzy against the wall. Still reeling from the prongs of the fork in her foot, she couldn't move to strike back.

When he pulled her shorts off her and put them over her face, she knew there was no point in fighting him. He'd smother her.

Dizzy went limp, tears streaming down her face as her own brother held her shorts over her nose and mouth. She couldn't gasp for air, let alone scream. No one would help, anyway, they were too far outside the city limits for there to be anyone to care.

When he finally let the cloth drop, she gasped. He was still at it. Crummie turned her, stomach to the wall. Searing pain as something cold and jagged went inside. A broken bottle. She looked up at the full moon high in the sky, and more tears slid down her face.

The sun rose and Dizzy broke free as Crummie fell to the floor in exhaustion. On shaky legs, she hobbled to the bathroom and cleaned up the mess. The woman in the mirror looked tired. Far away, she heard a mourning dove.

Maybe Miss Ladybird would understand that the girls really should take in Crummie and let him do stuff to the girls there. She could go there later when her bum and who felt better—maybe talk to her about it or something.

"You don't have the guts," the woman in the mirror said.

Dizzy fell to the floor and cried.

KERN

"You gotta know where the good places are around here— where to buy your smokes, your coke, and your pussy," Crummie said to the big, beefcake guy with the scar over his eye. He lit his hand rolled cigarette with a match from a bright purple book. The book was stamped with kissing lips, in black. ' Lipstick Atomic.'

"That third one didn't even rhyme," Kern said.

Crummie handed him the matchbook.

"Doesn't have to, pussy goes with everything."

Kern's old Army bearing didn't leave his face. He stared at Crummie until Crummie looked away at the horizon.

"You're a pig," Kern said.

"Oink-o boink-o," Crummie made a squealing noise and laughed like it was the greatest joke in the world. His lack of two front teeth made a whistling noise as he laughed.

Kern grunted.

This place disgusted Kern. The world disgusted Kern.

When he was a boy, his grandmother told him that people had always been scurrying, pathetic creatures trying to make ends meet, and now through his old man eyes he could see they were the same. Pathetic and struggling until they died.

Gram was 66 when she told him that. He was 66 now. He was 22 when she died. She was one of the lucky ones at ground zero. He had been deployed Over There. That was Big Day—the day that seventeen cities were hit from Over There.

44 years later, what was left was a false semblance of law, mostly anarchy states, and scarcity.

But here, Crummie, a young man trying too hard to impress an old soldier, was telling him this place was different. It was elevated. Not literally. They were at sea level. Most places were since The Great Rise.

"So what are you looking for? New Crescent City has everything—whores, smokes, weed, faggots if you're into shit-pokin', lotsa food and fresh meats. You gotta name it, man. I mean you're kinda old so maybe whores and fags aren't your thing—"

Kern snapped one hand out and seized Crummie by the throat, pulling him upward to look straight into his eyes.

"Stop talking."

Tears sprang out of Crummie's eyes and he tried to swallow. Kern could feel the Adam's apple slide against his palm. He reduced the pressure enough so that Crummie could answer in a small squeak. "Yes, sir."

Kern let go and leaned down so that his face was directly in Crummie's. " All right. Now answer me straight. I want a beer, a steak, and a place to relax—one where I can spend the night. What's the currency here?"

Crummie tried not to cower but Kern could see he was shaking. " T—the currency is credits, sir. King Louie's. If you don't have Kings, you can barter with work or with what you hunt. But, sir?"

"What?" Kern didn't offer relief in that stare. One more stupid comment and Crummie was going to be next on his hit list.

"You're a soldier. You get free stuff in exchange for protection from the Rabids."

"So New Crescent City's got a Rabids problem, I take it."

Crummie nodded.

"Course it does." Kern straightened up and looked around at the dinge and grime of the city. He was old enough to remember the old Crescent City (with all its dinge and grime) and when everyone fled after the third category five to hit in one summer. Anyone who stayed had been overrun by the Rabids.

Those were the nastiest results of a government experiment gone wrong. Oh sure, when that government existed they claimed it was natural causes, but after the head of the CIA put a bullet in her head just after concluding her live stream, the secret of the Rabids was out. They did it. They were responsible.

But with all chaos came those who were to restore order, and Kern was one of the order restorers. They weren't the preppers, they weren't the nutso ones wanting to restore any supremacy of any race. They were the Army. The new Army. And he'd been their commander until it was time to walk away. Once most states drew their new lines, their new boundaries, 55-year-old Kern took his final walk out the door.

Eleven years of mercenary work and earning those credits, he had come home. Not his real home. No, that had been gone for 44 years.

New Crescent City was the replacement for the old— where he'd met Del when they were just 11 years old, married and enlisted (both of them) right out of high school—and where they'd buried their newborn son. When he deployed, she had been given orders to stay in old CC and await further instructions.

That was the last he'd ever heard from her. They'd declared her dead. Dead with the rest of old Crescent City.

This home, not his home. What passion Kern had in him died the day Delphine did.

"Sir?"

"What now?"

"I was just gonna say, if you're looking for a place to stay and you've got credits, you can go to Lipstick Atomic. They have boarders there and Lady Beaumont runs the place."

Kern almost smiled at that last name—a common one for the area, but still, Delphine Beaumont had always managed to make him grin. He felt the dearth of her absence, ever since they were young, and he had moved on, but never so much looked at another person romantically again.

His job was his life for the next 44 years.

" Show me the place."

Crummie pointed away from the memorial grounds towards the street.

"Just past this neutral ground and over the hill. It's the main pit stop for travelers. If you'd kept walking you would've found it yourself."

Kern gave him a slight nod and started walking. Crummie followed.

"Hey—you gotta pay the toll for the memorial. Six credits."

The old man grunted and pulled out his digital minder, paying the little puke his due. Crummie grinned. "Great —with my share I can get a whore for the night."

Kern growled and stalked off. Crummie bounced after him.

"Hey you know what? I can come with you, maybe get you arranged for something permanent here if you want."

Kern stopped and turned, jabbing his finger at Crummie's face. " If you follow me, I'll blow your legs off."

Crummie backed away as Kern left for Lipstick Atomic.

"Okay, sir—maybe I'll see you there sometime." He gave him a sheepish smile, again flashing his two missing front teeth. Kern wondered who knocked them out and why they didn't finish the job.

Kern arrived in front of a ramshackle but functional hotel-slash-bordello that looked like it should have been in the middle of Vegas (Old Vegas, not the crater it became). It looked like it once tried to be a glorious cathouse. Twinks, androgynous attractive NBs and buxom women stood outside and tried to entice Kern as he made it to the door.

The inside was reminiscent of the old stripper houses Del threatened to buy and build up when they retired from the Army. Shining floors, neon lights, and bouncing tits everywhere. Nicer than the outside of the place, too (the décor, not the tits). Ebony wood and polished brass at the bar—and the scents of tobacco, spice, and perfumes made him take a deep breath. Loud music piped through the sound system as the women danced, some naked, some getting there.

Kern sat at the bar at the far end and focused on the woman behind it. She was somewhere in her 40s and reminded him of a cat.

"Stout and a steak, a pack of smokes, an ounce of nuggets, and a room for the night—alone," he said to the bartender. She was young, still somewhere between 45 to 50, but they looked younger to him every year.

"Thirty credits for the deal," she said. "You got King Louie's?"

He paid for the lot. She served him his stout, rolled the pack of smokes for him and handed him the bag of weed. He pocketed the smokes and baggie. Kern looked around over his shoulder, then back to the bar.

"Steak comes with green beans and potatoes. We have chocolate cake, too."

Kern nodded. " How much?"

"Two credits a slice, but they're big slices."

"Okay."

He paid for that too, added a tip, and drank his stout. Kern opened a tab.

About the third stout in, one familiar face appeared in the mirror above the bar. That dingbat Crummie was there, and he was half in the bag already. Kern finished his meal and went up to his room, falling asleep on top of the covers. At least the place was sort-of clean. Cleaner than he was.

He didn't want to dream, but as he drifted, he felt it coming to him. Not enough booze and weed in the world could keep the wars away.

Wars. Not just the Kill-Switch, but the decades after. His dream tonight decided to take him to his twenties.

Young father, they told him. A baby boy. He could go home soon to Crescent City. See his soldier wife and his little round-faced son. Del sent pictures and when it was his turn to use the internet at the encampment, he got to see his boy. The call was too short. Little Jake. Baby Jake. Kern sang him a song and he gaped at the screen as Del pointed and said, "that's your Daddy."

Dream Kern reached out to touch the screen, and when he withdrew his hand, it was covered in blood.

And the explosions started.
Shells whistled and blew up all around him.
He sought cover. Then, the dream took him ahead in time. Sitting at a desk at a Combat Army Surgical Hospital.

"You're cleared back for the field—but first, we have bad news. There's no good way to say it. Crescent City is gone."

"Gone?"

He wasn't in his own body anymore. He was looking at himself from the doorway, looking at the head surgeon, the fucking Colonel giving him the bad news. Kern saw his own stony face. He didn't look twenty-something to himself. He looked ancient. Even older than he was now.

"Wiped out by a nuclear warhead. I'm sorry, son. The CC is in the Gulf, and I'm sorry to say, we couldn't recover Delphine and Jake. I'm sorry."

Kern watched himself sit. Watched himself cry. Watched the Colonel stand there doing nothing but offer him a box of tissues. He turned and ran from the room, leaving them behind, to the middle of a field.

Rabids.

The Rabids surrounded their squad, and the nine of them, armed with flamethrowers and full tactical gear with rebreathers, sprayed the fields down as the swarms closed in. The buzzing sound they always made echoed in his ears and made his teeth rattle. So many of them. Would they lift out in time? Could they lift out in time?

He watched Bucky, a leg fresh out of basic, get snatched up by a swarm. He watched as the horde tore him to pieces. Kern blasted them with his flamethrower, but it was too late for Bucky.

And when they removed his gas mask, his infant son was there, crying as the Rabids tore him apart. He cried out and thrashed in bed, sweat breaking out in fat beads on his forehead. Kern knocked over the side table and the booze clattered to the floor.

When he woke, the place was quiet. Dark. He checked his watch. It was sunset when he arrived at Atomic Lipstick, but now it was 0400.

Except for the sounds of fucking, cucking, and muffled screaming. The music was no longer a thrumming beat into his dreams. Instead, it was a late night jazz club playing softer beats as if the place were singing a lullaby to itself.

Kern assumed the muffled screaming was some hardcore dominatrix, mashing her cigarettes out on the chest of a sub. The thought made him laugh. He scrounged around for ear plugs, found them in his rucksack. After a bowl and a fifth of the bottle of bourbon he'd bought, he was back to sleep. He planned to talk to the owner in the morning about possible work for an old soldier.

The things he overheard that night about Lady (short for Ladybird) Beaumont made him wonder if she was a cousin of Del's. Lady was good at poker, good at shooting, good at keeping the staff healthy, making them get regular STI checks. They called her a silver fox, wondered when she would make an appearance for a poker tourney, or if she'd host a snooker with hookers night again.

From those floating conversations among the dancers, bartenders, and jack-holes all around him, he gathered that this Lady person was about his age, had some kind of forces training so she could handle her own security, and built an empire in King Louie's Territory.

She was off somewhere doing business in the Haggle Huts —a spot in the southernmost part of the territory where people traded their wares and services—and would be back with supplies to keep the place going. Savvy and sharp, they said. Took care of the young ones and never let anyone stay down on their luck, but woe betide the asshole who messed with any of her girls.

Protective. Like his Del had been.

As his thoughts carried him back to sleep, he dreamt of the way things had been for them. They knew where the world was going, but together, they would fight for something better.

When they sent her home to have their newborn, they knew he would be born into war. What they didn't know was that he'd be born into the end of the world and he would go with it.

This world took a long time to die. Lots longer than he thought it would. Turned out humans sucked at that, too. 44 years since the world took Del from him, and it still didn't have the decency to get struck by a meteor.

Well, it was almost 2090. Maybe they'd hit the ELE Bingo then.

A knock on his door woke him. Kern jumped out of bed.

"Rabids! Everyone get to the safety shelter now," came a woman's voice. Cherise, the bartender? Sounded like it might be her.

Rabids were the main concern, he thought as he grabbed his rifle. He had his hunting knife with its nine-inches of solid steel and his long arm. He'd be fine. The Rabids wouldn't.

He threw open the door. "I don't seek shelter," he said, then stopped.

The dancers and sex workers were shooting out the window at an approaching wave of Rabids. Rabids swarmed, the best way being to spread their illness via close contact, and the only way to keep them from spreading further was to kill them as quickly as possible, which is what these women were doing. Some were interrupted from their work (coitus interruptus by swarmus, he thought as he ran to one of the top floor windows), but they were shooting with military precision, not wasting ammo and clearing headshot after headshot.

Kern jumped into the fray, choosing one of the unguarded windows. He gauged where it would be best to shoot— where the others weren't clearing out. The swarms were part of the virus. These weren't zombies or anything like the movies ever showed—they were still perfectly alive and hearty. But they weren't human.

They didn't problem solve. They just... swarmed and were violent.

Waves of Rabids approached and Kern watched as heads exploded, skulls cracking open, some exploding in a burst of gray matter and skull fragments, some with perfect round holes in the forehead and dropping to the ground to be trampled. He found a patch that was still able to advance and began to spray them down.

When he ran out of ammo, he reassessed.

More were coming.

Cherise, the bartender, was at another window kitty-corner to him. She had been laughing—no—cackling as she fired from her Mx4 Storm, mowing down throngs of Rabids. She ran out of ammo.

More were coming.

"Time to flip the bitch switch!" Cherise ran down the stairs to the bar and hauled out a remote detonator. "

"Everybody down!"

Man, that woman could bellow. With her two-tone blue and purple hair and a mouth big enough to shout down the building, she could've been Del's kin. Kern ducked as she ordered, but watched from shielded eyes as the wave of Rabids got hit with perimeter traps that sprung from the ground. They fell into the pits in globs.

The bartender whooped and hollered, then pressed the red button in the center and— Nothing happened.

"Shit," Cherise slammed the detonator down on the bar and tried again, but nothing happened. The bodies stacked on top of each other in the pits. " Goddamn it."

In the distance, more reports. Kern looked in the direction of the noise to see a woman with a shotgun and an eye patch. What, really, an eye patch? No, sunglasses. She was blowing the Rabids away. Bodies climbing off the pits, using other Rabids as weight, turned to try to aim for the woman, to consume her in their rabid violence and unending hunger.

Kern shook his head. Her form—tall and slender (and so familiar)—came closer, but he couldn't make out much about her. Short, silver hair, a shotgun, and a cigar. He couldn't make out the details of her face. His vision wasn't that eagle-eyed anymore.

"That's Ladybird," Cherise said from below. " I recognize that swagger anywhere."

Kern squinted and tried to get a better look. There was a moment where his heart felt like it was doing triple time, but settled as he refocused on ways to form a rescue if she got overwhelmed. He started to leave, all the way downstairs. Cherise put her arm out and stopped him.

"No, sir—come on over here and watch Ladybird work."

He stopped and joined Cherise by the window. Though he couldn't see her face anymore (she'd covered it with a bandana), he could see she'd moved with lightning speed closer to the pits. But not too close. She was taunting the Rabids.

In one hand, her shotgun still. In the other, something like a cell phone, but as she drew nearer and the Rabids came closer, she put the object over her head.

A detonator? No shit.

FWOOM.

Kern was familiar with the sounds of many kinds of IEDs but these? These were the work of a professional. The bodies, or pieces of bodies, flew into the air and all around, geysers of blood spewing from the pits. It looked like someone was blending Bloody Marys and left the top off the blender.

As parts rained down all around them outside, Kern lost sight of the woman completely.

It got quiet. The buzzing moans and cries of Rabids, gone.

"We've got to go out there," Kern said.

Before Cherise could respond, the door burst open and Kern prepared for a surprise horde of Rabids. But it wasn't any Rabid. It was Ladybird, covered in gore, clothes torn from grappling with Rabids, and a wicked grin around that damn cigar.

"Hoo-ee, son! Those Rabids got barbecued today, n'est-ce pas?"

"Del?" Kern said. The voice was hers, though rough and husky from years of chain smoking and hollering, he was sure of it.

Del pulled down her bandana and looked at him, mouth hanging open. "John? They told me you were dead."

"They told me the same."

This wasn't a cue the violins moment, though he wanted it to be. He wanted to pick her up and kiss her, swing her around, and take her upstairs all at once. But there was no time.

Never was any time for them, it seemed. Not in 44 years. He opened his mouth to say something, to tell her he never let her go or something as equally sentimental, but...

"There's a swarm incoming again," Cherise announced this from the window as the other women brought in crates full of ammo.

Del grabbed a box of shells for her shotgun and shook her head. "Guess we'll chit-chat later, soldier. Now get to your station."

She started barking orders and the women and Twinks did as they were told. Kern kept sneaking glances at her as she worked.

"Y'all, I got to reset the traps later. For now, looks like it's a small swarm. Spray 'em down and set 'em free."

Kern set his sights on his section and readied himself for when they crossed the territory line.

As soon as they got past the outside gates, it would be too late. They waited until the Rabids hit the neutral ground. Once they were there, Del gave the command to fire.

They swept up as fast as they had started, and as sunset came, Crescent City cleanup crews were digging bodies out of pits.

Reunited under bloodshed. Bloodshed, the way they had intended to go out—shooting up the Over-Theres and going out in a rain of mortars. That hadn't been how it turned out. Maybe now they'd get their chance.

CRUMMIE RETURNS

Crummie had fun making fun of people. Sometimes it got him punched but most of the time he was bigger and meaner, so getting into fights was just fine.

Now with Kern hanging around, there was someone bigger on the block, but hey, since he made friendly-like with the guy and practically got him the job there, the girls might be more friendly to him. Didn't matter. He was paying, so he got to say what they did and how they liked it.

He was so hard it was painful by the time he walked in, making no effort to hide it. One of the new girls was doing it to him. He'd seen her a couple weeks ago but wasn't allowed to go in. Lady had knocked out his two front teeth when she kicked him out. Old bitch had a right hook that could break jaws.

She'd warned him off, too. He wasn't allowed back or she'd kill him, but all the girls had final say because of some shit like ' your body, your choice.' Besides, he had credits and paid them.

Ladybird was busy with Kern, though. He'd heard all about it—he thought his wife was dead and she thought he was dead and it'd been 44 years since they'd seen each other. Before he was born, even. But that was keeping her distracted, catching up with him and spending time alone with him. Cherise was in charge too but he could sneak by her because she was busy at the bar.

The new girl noticed him watching one of the girls dance and could see his erection pitching a tent and no not one of those pup-tents either. His dick was huge, his other sister said so before she died choking on it.

That had been fun. He forced his sister to go down on him and held her head there as she choked on it. Even when she bit down it hurt but it was funny, too. He took the ice pick he liked to carry and stabbed it behind her ear.

She didn't clamp down on it after that, and he fucked the noise hole until it grew cold. He made Dizzy bury her in the garden near Momma and Daddy.

The thought made him laugh to himself as the new girl approached. He gave her his friendliest smile and invited her to sit with him at the table.

"Hey, sugar," New Girl said. " Welcome to Lipstick Atomic. You look thirsty, can I get you a bevvy on the house?"

He held up his liter of pale lager, some of the cheapest swill that would get him drunk, and shook it at her. " I already paid so you can credit me back if you wanna."

She smiled and giggled. " Well I tell you what, next one's on the house for a cutie like you."

He grinned big at that. Most of the other girls ignored him or just got down to business if they were desperate for credits. Those were the ones with problems and scars, either from coming close to losing battles with Rabids, or from the wars that preceded the Rabids Uprising.

The New Girl seemed pretty promising—as long as Crummie could keep her from talking to the others. He handed over his keeper. " Tell you what. How about we just go right upstairs and skip the drink? I could have it later. I'd much rather have you."

The eyes—her eyes—hungry for some money, sure, but maybe even hungry for a piece of him. He grinned as she took her share. They headed up the stairs to her room.

"My name's Leda—what's yours?" She asked, giving him a smile.

"Crummie. But I didn't ask your name and I don't give a fuck," he said, then laughed, unzipping his trousers.

The smile fell from her face. " Well, I gotta check you before we start. Did you give your STI report when you came in?"

"Shut up. I'm clean. Ain't been with no one dirty." Crummie stepped closer to her and she let him. That was enough of an invitation.

"I still have to check you out. Ladybird says always check, so that's what we do."

He slapped her in the face and she flinched.

"No, I don't do the rough stuff," she said.

Crummie laughed. " You do when I say you do," he said. His head was a little swimmy, the way he liked it when he was drinking more than he should.

"I said ` no`." Leda swatted his hand away.

That only served to piss him off. He gripped her hand in his and squeezed it until he heard the familiar popping sound of dislocation. She whimpered and drew in a breath to scream.

He clamped one hand over her mouth and pushed her down, putting his knee between her legs. His hand slid down to wrap around her throat. " You scream and I break your fucking neck. Got it?"

Leda nodded. She looked around the room and Crummie could see she was searching for something. A weapon, maybe. He knew this wasn't going to be easy—but come on, he paid for it, this was rightfully his. She didn't get to choose.

Crummie balled up his fist and connected it to the side of her head. He heard a meaty thud and a soft crackling of gristle as the skin on her cheek popped open. A rivulet of blood ran down the side of her face. Her eyes rolled, then closed as she went limp.

Fine, Crummie thought. Better her being limp than me. He laughed out loud as if she might have appreciated the joke, then went to work getting his money's worth. And when he finally went limp, he grabbed a beer bottle, smashed it, and marked his territory all over her lower lips, cut after cut, leaving glass fragments behind and inside.

LADYBIRD

Delphine " Ladybird" Beaumont had no tolerance for fools. After 44 years of rebuilding her life, of mercenary work, of helping to rebuild a new city, of carving out a niche, buying off the new law—here she was.

Sitting across from Kern in her brothel/strip joint/hotel.

"The reality hasn't hit yet," Del said. " They told me they never recovered your body. I guess they told you the same."

Kern nodded. " What do we do now?"

She tossed back another shot of whiskey and poured out another round. " Same shit, I guess. I mean—we could use your skills for protection."

"You've been doing fine on your own for—however long you've been doing this. You don't need me." Kern shrugged.

"No, not `need` you, but I want you around. Guess we just have to get used to each other again." She smiled. " I think you'll prevent a lot of problems. I mean, look at you. You're huge and intimidating. I'm the only one who's ever seen you smile, for fuck's sake."

He laughed. As they finished their breakfast, there was a knock at the door—one knock followed by four quick raps. Kern put his hand over his sidearm but Del shook her head. " That's one of my employees. Secret knock."

She opened it and Leda fell forward into Del's arms, sobbing. Del pulled her into a hug and shut the door with one foot. " Come on, sugar. Let's get you sat. There's a seat right here."

Leda resisted sitting for a moment, hyperventilating. "I ca—can't sit, it hurts, it hurts."

But she managed to lean to the side and rested her hip on the chair, wincing.

Delphine could smell the rancid stench of old sweat and grime on her—a scent she was far too familiar with from having to deal with that little asshole on more than one occasion. Still, she waited for Leda to calm down enough to talk.

"Kern, pour her a cup of coffee, put a shot of brandy in it, steel her nerves," Del said. Kern did as he was told.

Once Leda finished telling her what happened, and lifting her cover up to show her the broken skin and elongated cuts that still had pieces of glass sticking out of them, she looked at Del with a shamed face. " I shouldn't have let him in, I know. It's my fault."

"No, sugar, it's his fault. But don't you worry, we're gonna set this right. First off, we're gonna call Doc Cross and get you cleaned up, then Kern here's gonna take a ride to the old ranch off Pertwee Extension and make a pickup. And while we wait, you and I are gonna make up some plans."

She held the young woman's face in her hands and wiped her tears. A moment of maternal affection turned to Gorgon-like fury as she stood and met Kern eye-to-eye. " Go down to the ranch, the only one with a big garden out front at the end of Pertwee Extension, grab Crummie out of his house and deliver him here. Cherise will show you where to deposit him."

Kern nodded and headed out. When Ladybird gave an order, everyone listened.

Delphine told Cherise to call Doc Cross for a health check and assault cleanup, no cops. Even if the shit police around these parts showed up it was either to fuck or take a bribe. Same as it ever was.

"Once the good Doc has come to check you out and get your glass out, you can work behind the bar or dance while you recover. If and when you're ready to get back in the saddle, you can. But tonight, I'll show you how we handle scum like Crummie."

Leda's tears dried up, she finished her coffee and brandy and waited for the doctor. Ladybird went to the back room. She had some setting up to do.

RETRIEVAL

Dizzy kept her door locked ever since that night Crummie came home early. This night had been no different. Even though she was pretty sure he was at Lipstick Atomic and he probably got lucky.

And she sure wasn't going to answer whoever it was pounding on the door. She jumped out of bed and cowered near the window, ready to hop out if whoever it was burst through to her bedroom.

Getting brave enough to peek out her window, she popped up like a meerkat and looked to the front door. There was a man—he was big and rough-looking with scars on his face and bullet wounds all over his arms. He rapped on the door again. " Crummie! Come on out or I'm coming in."

Was he really here to get Crummie? She hopped up and ran to the door, throwing it open. " Crummie's not here," she said. " It's just me. Crummie's up at Lipstick Atomic."

"No, he's not," the big man said. " That's where I just came from. Who the hell are you?"

"Dizzy," she said.

"You should sit down," he said.

"No—I mean my name's Dizzy," she said. " You?"

"Kern."

"What do you want with Crummie?"

Kern raised his eyebrows. "Is he here?"

"I don't know—I didn't think he came in last night. You can come in and look for him, though."

Kern shook his head. " I see he's earned your loyalty too, huh?"

Dizzy shrugged and Kern scowled as he made his way inside. From the corner of her eye, she saw movement. A flash of his long and scraggly hair. "Hope you find him," she said.

For once, Crummie wouldn't be able to say anything back without getting caught. Dizzy didn't smile. There would be no gloating over this victory.

She left to tend the garden.

While she was busy with the onions, Dizzy heard a scream that didn't belong to the gruff man—it was far too high-pitched. No, that was the unmistakable squeal of her pig brother. She turned to look at the house in time to see Kern dragging a hog-tied Crummie out the door and down the long drive to the Extension.

She smiled, allowing herself a sliver of relief as she looked over at the mounds where her parents were buried and sighed. Maybe now, they could all rest. Whatever Crummie did, he'd pay. Maybe she'd be lucky and never see him again.

Dizzy started walking toward Lipstick Atomic, following a feeling that she should pay them a visit.

JUDGMENT

Kern dragged Crummie behind him and looked to the bar at Cherise. She gave Kern a big smile and waved him over to her. " Well lookie here at what the big cat done dragged in."

"Where should I take him?" Kern asked. Crummie didn't say anything, because Crummie was still unconscious.

There weren't many customers yet, some were just leaving from their overnight checks, and no dancers meant no bar patrons. The ones who were lingering in the main room chuckled at the state of the young man or looked away.

"The back office. It's all the way down the hall where it says staff only. There's a little sloping floor downward to the basement. Well, the pseudo-cellar. Closest thing we have to one around these parts." Cherise motioned him to follow her.

"You know, everyone thought you were dead," she said as they walked down the long hallway.

"I recovered."

She laughed. "Lots of us were thought to be dead—most of us just wanted to be."

Cherise opened the door for him and then left his side as Del greeted him with a smile. She had a pair of pliers in her hand. A chair, bolted to the floor, sat in the center of the room. It was old, and metal. It looked like an electric chair.

Crummie came to and struggled to break free from Kern, but his eyes widened and he shrieked when he saw Ladybird. His eyes darted from the chair, to Ladybird and her pliers, then back again.

"Shut your mouth," Del said. Then, to Kern:

"Sit him in the chair and strap him in."

He took orders from his General. In a few swift moves, Crummie was seated.

"All nice and cozy," she said. She motioned for Kern to move back. He did, choosing a spot in the corner where he'd be out from underfoot.

"Wait, Lady Beaumont, please—there's been a big mistake," Crummie said.

Ladybird laughed. " Oh, yes, there's been a huge mistake. Mine."

She came down with a hard punch, connecting to Crummie's lips. And as the copper tang of blood filled his mouth, he noticed with chagrin that she'd knocked out all his front teeth this time. He spat them out onto the floor.

" Now, my first mistake was not doing this two months ago when you started acting like a creep around my staff, but I thought you were young yet,

still trying to figure out the type of man you wanted to be. Well, you made a choice, didn't you?"

Crummie's mouth moved but the words didn't follow.

"Come on, Crummie—you can talk, I didn't hit you that hard," she said. " I can try again if you want to know how a hard hit feels."

Crummie felt the inside of his mouth—when Ladybird hit him, his back teeth caught and clamped down on his tongue. Throbbing and swelling started fast, but he gathered his voice and brought his eyes up to meet hers.

"I paid for her—she has to do what I say when I pay," Crummie's speech was slurred and trickles of blood ran from his mouth as he spoke. " That's what whores are for."

"You know damn well that's not how it works, shit-heels," she said. She turned away and fished through a large steel box. Crummie pulled against his metal restraints, but all it did was cut into his wrists and ankles.

"Kern? Strap his chest in too," Ladybird said, handing him the chains. " He's not going anywhere."

"Kern did as he was told and then backed off again. Watching Delphine Beaumont work had been a pleasure then, and now.

She emerged from the steel box with several tools in hand, including a metal mouth spreader and props. With Crummie's front teeth broken, Kern knew what was coming next.

As Del began her work, she met Crummie's pleading gaze with a deadpan stare. She took the mouth spreader and forced it into him. Then, the metal props, holding his mouth open for him so he couldn't bite down.

One by one, the teeth came out and went into a jar with a collection of other teeth. Plink, plink, plink. Years of teeth. Some had fillings. Some were broken and suffered decay. All of them had blood stains on them. Crummie screamed with each removal, and passed out when she put her foot on his chest and pulled out the final back tooth.

"Smelling salts," she said. She held out one hand soaked in blood.

Kern provided the ammonium salts from his First-Aid Kit. Del snatched the salts from him and broke open the plastic ampoule under Crummie's nose.

He came to, whimpering.

"Please, stop. I won't do it again, promise," he said—except it came out as " Pwease, stop. I won't do it again, pwomise." It made Kern laugh. Crummie didn't look over at him.

Crummie gave Ladybird a pleading look but she was unfazed, gazing down on him. She appeared to consider something. One corner of her mouth turned up in a sly half-smile.

"No, you won't do it again," she said. That bloody hand fished around in her pocket and drew out a pack of rolled cigarettes. She put one in her mouth and lit it. " You certainly won't do it again. Kern?"

"Yes, ma'am?"

"Take his clothes off him and burn them—Cherise will take them out and do it. I don't want a lice infestation," she said.

"I'll be back in a few minutes."

"Yes, ma'am," Kern said. He didn't ask where she was going, or what she was doing. Even after all these years, he trusted her.

Kern took scissors and cut Crummie out of his clothing, ignoring the young man's pleas for help, offering bribes, and figuratively pissing himself to get out of the chair. Based on Crummie's reaction, he knew what was coming. Maybe not exactly what—not all of the details—but he knew this was not something he'd survive.

"Look, Kern—I mean it. I won't even come around here. I'll move away. I'll leave town. You can't let her come back here. You can't let her do this to me."

Kern made the final cut into Crummie's waistband and pulled the wad of clothes off him, now wasted rags in his fist. He tossed them to the middle of the concrete floor, found the cloth bag to put them in, and opened the door. Cherise was there with a shotgun. She took the clothing, and then barked to another one of the women to put them in the burn barrel.

He slammed the door, making Crummie jump.

"Please," Crummie said, crying harder. " I don't deserve what I'm gonna get."

"Quit whining," Kern said. He moved back to face Crummie. " You deserve everything you get."

"I don't wanna die, I don't wanna, I don't wanna—"

Kern drew back his fist and landed a square hit against Crummie's face. A gunshot crack of a breaking nose responded, and blood gushed from his face. Crummie screamed.

"Shut up, it's not that bad," Kern said. He grabbed a clean rag from a nearby shelf and stuck it to Crummie's face. Crummie coughed and gagged, then was still. He'd passed out again. Kern waited.

Crummie came to consciousness and looked up at him.

"It is that bad. You don't know. You don't know what it's like."

"Christ, kid—be a man instead of a whining little brat. You had a real chance here. A last chance. You've probably never lived a day in your life like a man should."

He didn't usually say this much, but, after a thoughtful pause, added: " At least you have the chance to die like one."

Crummie scowled but with his busted nose, all it made him do was whimper.

Kern wondered what Del had in mind for this one. As the clock ticked its beats, Kern observed. Beneath the sounds of Crummie's whimpering and occasional moan, he couldn't hear anything outside of the doors.

Soundproof. Damn. She'd spared no expense building this place up. He couldn't hear the music let alone any sort of conversation or noise outside. Given the placement of the chair, the drains on the floor, and the easy-to-clean tiled walls, this room was built for this kind of thing.

The door behind him opened and two women entered —Ladybird and Leda. Behind them, Cherise was greasing up a lawman. He saw the woman give him something—drugs, it looked like—then the door shut before he could see the rest of the transaction. Money. Probably the more untraceable currencies. Things were easier to hide in this world than they were when he was younger. Corruption was everywhere, and it was just like Ladybird to take advantage of it and carve out her own niche for it.

Better her brand of lawful lawlessness than Crummie's.

Del was carrying a large toolbox. Leda was carrying a bucket full of Tetra-5xy, a compound that was impossible to come by after the dissolution of the first military. It took an expert to make it successfully without blowing up a place, and had to be stored in metal buckets. Contact with skin caused immediate necrosis, and the only way to remove it was to burn it off.

Kern saw a company hit with Tetra, coming to their rescue. They had to abort the mission, but Kern remembered the stench of rotting flesh as the entire company turned to necrotic goop before his eyes. His team had been spared, but some of them couldn't stop puking from the stench.

Both Leda and Del (he would rarely ever think of her as Ladybird) wore full protective gear, and Del tossed him a face mask and eye protection. " Stand over in the corner, darlin'," she said.

Kern nodded and did so.

"What do you want to do first, Leda?" Del asked.

"Weedah, I'm sowwy," Crummie said. "Puh-puh-please don't hurt me. I pwah—" he stopped here and gathered himself so he could speak clearly. " I promise it will never happen again. Lady Beaumont, I'll leave town. Anything."

Both women glared at him and he quieted. After the treatment Kern had given his face, and what Ladybird had done to his mouth, he knew there was no getting out of this. He wet himself.

"Slide the bottom out so it'll drain," Del said to Kern. He stepped over, knelt down, and found the latches to free the bottom. Urine spilled onto the floor and down the slope to the center drain.

Leda's face behind the protective gear was passive on the surface, but it was a mask. A thin mask. There was nothing but contempt and rage in her eyes. " Doc says I'm going to be out of commission for at least three weeks while I heal," she said. " There was more glass inside, too. She gave me a numbing agent and she had to stitch me up in a couple places."

Del waited. It wasn't the answer to the question, but the answer was coming as Leda talked it over with herself.

"This. This is what I want to do to him," she said, holding up the bucket of Tetra. " But do your thing first, Lady Beaumont. Show me the equalizer."

With a somber nod, Del set the toolbox down with a loud clatter and opened it. She extracted a clamp, a bottle of cinnamon hot lubricant, and a tool that looked an awful lot like a potato peeler, but a high-end tungsten steel blade. It looked like it had heft.

She covered her gloves in the lube. With clinical precision, Delphine bathed Crummie's sword in it until it was ready for the forge. Crummie, still crying, begged her to stop. She didn't. Once she had him at full mast, she applied the clamp. It kept blood flow to the area, and the skin turned a deep shade of purple.

"Madam Beaumont, please, that hurts. Please stop. You don't want to hurt me," he said.

"Don't presume to tell me what I want, you little fuck-wit," she said.

"You didn't have a problem with hurting me at all," Leda added.

"I—I don't want to do this. Please—I'll find a way to make it up to you. To all of you," Crummie said.

"We're way past that, sugar," Del said. " Besides, I left you alone to get something arranged just for you.

Well, not just for you, for my girls, too. And someone who's been putting up with your bullshit for far too long."

She turned away from Crummie. " Kern, open the door and ask Cherise to bring in my special surprise."

Again, Kern followed Del's instructions to the letter. Cherise greeted him with a big smile, and sent in the surprise.

Dizzy entered the room. She was clean, wearing a neat floral print dress and a yellow sun hat. She looked younger than she did the last time Kern saw her. Almost like a little kid. He felt like she shouldn't see something like this.

"Dizz, what? What are you doing here?" Crummie said. His eyes were swelling shut from the blow Kern delivered earlier.

Dizzy got in closer. " I'm here to help," she said. She held out her hand to Del. " Lady Beaumont?"

"What is it, sweetest one?"

"On the nights he got turned away, he'd come home drunk. He would either beat me up or force himself on me. Night after night. He liked to stick things up there when he was done. Humiliate me. Make me bleed."

"I never did that," Crummie said. " You're my sister. That's not allowed."

Dizzy's eyes were shining. She ignored him, still looking at Lady Beaumont. She took a shaky breath, and steadied herself. " So many nights I would look out the kitchen window and wait for the moon to set. I begged the gods that he'd cross you and get shot. I got a dog to maybe protect myself. Her name was Squiggles."

Dizzy swallowed hard. " She was a beautiful blue tick hound. Big, soulful eyes. I loved her so much."

"I never met Squiggles," Lady Beaumont said, voice gentle. " Tell me. Let it out, baby girl."

Tears welled and she sniffled. At first, the words didn't want to come, but Dizzy drew in another breath. " He got drunk one night and came home. I was sleeping with Squiggles. Some nights she could scare him off."

But not that night," Leda said.

"No, not that night. He grabbed her by the collar and took her outside. She tried to bite him. I ran after them—tried to stop him. He beat her head in with a shovel and told me it was my fault. My fault for liking her better than I liked him." She sobbed.

Silence. Crummie coughed.

"But I want to help." Dizzy still held out her hand. " I'll take the tool."

"It's all yours, Miss Dizzy," Del said.

"Dizzy, please—don't. I promise I'm sorry. I promise!" Crummie said.

Dizzy didn't reply. The first peel of the foreskin was slow and determined, and came off easily.

Crummie screamed and the veins in his neck pulsed, tendons and cords standing out in contrast to the hollows of his throat. " No more, please, no more!"

But Dizzy was in a trance, fascinated by peeling the skin all the way around the glans and head until she had created a flesh flower, covered in blood.

Crummie kept screaming until he lost consciousness, but the clamp held him fast. Del continued to wake him with smelling salts as Dizzy kept peeling each layer. Dizzy finished with him and dropped the peeler on the floor. He passed out again. She slapped him across the face once. Twice. Three times.

He came back to consciousness and Dizzy moved in close, nose to broken nose. " And just think, Crummie—you still have Hell to look forward to."

She kissed the tip of his nose and he made a pained, gurgling sound like he wanted to say something, but all that came out was a bubble of blood. Dizzy snarled, rage lining her face and adding decades of age she had earned in less than two decades of life.

"Years of putting up with you. Years of your egotistic rants about how people should respect you and how you defended Momma and Daddy against the Rabids and that you almost died when it was ME defending them—you lying sack of shit—you'd do anything for attention, anything to get what you want, and now it's all caught up to you, and even through all that you STILL have the guts to try to talk back to me?"

Crummie smiled his toothless grin, and out spilled another runner of blood. " Yeah. You bitches bring it on yourselves. I don't deserve this, Dizz! I took care of you. I loved you!"

She backhanded him once. Twice. Hard. He stopped talking and started moaning, incoherent.

Dizzy turned to Ladybird. " I'm done. I'm going home. Do what you want with him, but I don't want to see him again."

As she turned to leave, Leda worked fast with the Tetra. She nodded to Ladybird. " I know what I need to do. Can you keep him awake?"

"Not a problem, sugar." She held up a pouch with a syringe. " But the salts can only do so much. So I'll use this. He'll be alert and still feel everything."

Kern didn't want to know what was in the syringe, but a memory of experimental serum came back to him. Something that was in the works for torture. In the Before. How she got her hands on it, well, his Del was always able to get things. It was one of her talents.

Leda waited and when Crummie was alert, she stepped up and painted the Tetra across his torso. The scent of decay filled the room as Crummie screamed, piling obscenities at her feet and wailing at the ceiling as his head snapped back.

"There," she said. She moved back to put the barrel aside and Kern saw what she had done. The word RAPIST, emblazoned in necrotic tissue, stood out on his chest as he continued to cry. It ate into his muscle. Soon, he would have a full hole of the word, exposing his sternum and ribs.

"No, no, this isn't happening," Crummie said. He wiggled around in the chair but all that served to do was make him hurt even more.

"Cherise? Get your pretty ass in here," Ladybird called.

Cherise, with the purple and blue hair. Cherise, with the big smile and big attitude, came into the room. " Yes, ma'am?"

It's time. He's still awake. Put him to bed."

She looked over at Kern. " You'll want hearing protection," she said. " On the shelf."

Leda left the room. Cherise, Kern, and Ladybird donned their noise-canceling hearing protectors. Cherise left the room for a moment and returned with her shotgun. Kern laughed. Their ears were still ringing from the Rabids earlier, but in this enclosed space, they'd go deaf. Del thought of everything.

Cherise looked to her Ladybird and Kern, making sure they were ready. As Crummie screamed, cried, and called them cunts, she squeezed the trigger.

Crummie's head parted, looking like a rose in full bloom as the jaw came unhinged and dangled from the side of his face. The lips, nose, and lower cheeks were open as flesh and muscle dripped from the bones and splattered onto his lap and the floor below.

"The best part is that his eyes look surprised," Kern said. Del—Ladybird—pointed to her ear protection and shook her head.

They removed their gear in near unison and Kern repeated himself. Ladybird laughed.

"We aim to deliver a surprising yet satisfying experience," she said. But the smile faded as she got back to business. " Cherise, let's get this cleaned up. Grinder, bring it out to the canal for the gators, all that. I'll save the torso."

Kern watched as they cut up Crummie, and Ladybird
took the torso to her workbench. "This'll go on the
fence as a warning. Patrons can behave themselves or
get marked," she said.

"You think that'll be good for business?" Kern asked.

"No—but it's good for the employees. They know
they're protected. Crummie wasn't welcome back here
and I should have done better to keep him out.
Should've taken care of him a long time ago," Ladybird
looked up from her work of scooping out the organs. " I
have a lot of regrets. One more to add to the pile, I
suppose."

Kern put his hand on her shoulder. She leaned into him.

"I'll clean up the rest. But what about the cops?"

"Ladybird is the law around here," she said. " What
police force we have left is a joke. They've always been
a joke—in old Crescent City, and the new one, too."

"Kern grabbed a mop and bleach, and got to work
cleaning up the remnants of revenge.

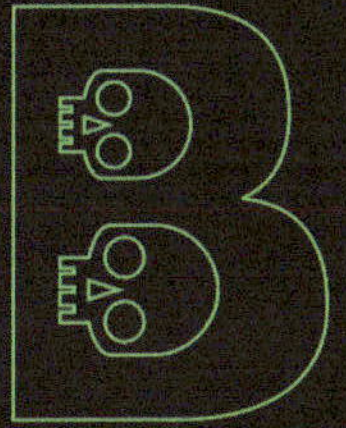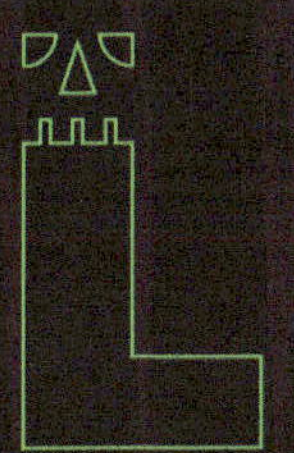

BLEED

by Michael Strong

Colonel Stevens led Galloway through the encampment towards a large tent. Relentless sunlight beat down upon them. Although the British Company's rule in India was no more, the beast still lived here in the African interior.

Behind the tent, blacker than it had any earthly right to be, a patch of fog sat atop the bright sands. The mass bled towards the sky in a crude column but was dense, not an aerosol like proper fog. Inky growths writhed from it like snakes from a gorgon's head.

Stevens held open a flap of the tent. Beneath Galloway's feet, the ground hummed whilst the mass made a wet sound, like someone slurped soup.

"Doctor Galloway, be seated," Stevens said and dropped the flap closed.

Jacob Galloway removed his pith helmet and sat. The British Company once clamoured for his services but he was forty now, a wind-up toy wound down, and no longer the commodity he'd once been. Perhaps opportunity knocked.

"We've misplaced a few of our scientists," Stevens said. "Can you help us retrieve them?"

"I'll need more information than that, Colonel. You've misplaced them how? Or rather, where?"

"250 men are lost in total. We sent a contingent into the mist five days ago to study resources. However, the Company's concern is to recover the scientists. The others are immaterial." After twenty years in the Company's employ, from India to Africa, Galloway understood 'sent a contingent' meant 'to leech the land dry'.

"Surely the Company is concerned with such a significant loss of manpower," Galloway said.

"They're mostly lascars, Doctor, waiting for ships. Profits come from scientific innovation—more addictive tobacco, stronger strains of tea, making workers more productive. The workforce is replaceable, the scientists are less so."

Stevens stood and motioned Jacob to follow. "We have one man who came back from the expedition. He's taken leave of his senses, the poor bastard, but he may be of some use to you." Galloway and Stevens walked towards another tent, this one smaller. Two armed guards saluted Stevens then held open the tent flaps. The black mass undulated behind them yet remained stationary somehow.

Why did the wind not take it elsewhere? Why did the heat not burn it up? Why did it gurgle and twist like an upset stomach?

Inside this tent, a man sat in a locked iron cage, the small enclosure more befitting a dog than a human. The man stank of sweat and rotten vegetation. Greasy ginger hair touched his shoulders and a tangled beard reached the centre of his chest.

"Doctor Darling, meet Doctor Galloway, who worked for us previously as a chemist," Stevens said, tone neutral but face pinched in unconscious distaste.

"How do you do, Doctor Darling?" Galloway asked. "In what branch of the sciences do you practise?"

"Botany," Darling said, voice ragged from disuse.

"We took sampl—"

The man's mouth quivered in an 'o' shape for a moment before he found his voice.

"You."

He scrambled to the corner of his cage farthest away from Galloway.

"You killed me." His voice crescendoed into a shout and he gripped the clots of his hair. "You killed us all!"

Galloway exchanged glances with Colonel Stevens, who shrugged one shoulder.

"We've never met before, when did I kill you?" Jacob said.

"On the other side." Darling's chest hitched and he began to weep. He hugged himself and rocked. "Y-you bled us dry, then came back for more. Murderer."

"We sent five scientists and 245 men into the mist to explore," Colonel Stevens said.

"We don't know what happened to the others, he's the only one to return, but I can attest to one thing. Doctor Darling was clean-shaven and had close-cropped hair when we sent them in five days ago."
Jacob dismissed this nonsense with a shake of his head.

Darling buried his face in his arms. "It wasn't five days, it was forever. I died a thousand times, then came back again. Things hunted us night after night. Beasts with cleavers and wings like leather, beasts that ate our insides."

Stevens ignored the botanist, face pale. "Can you recover the others, Doctor Galloway?"

"I'll find your scientists, Colonel Stevens, alive or dead. We shouldn't ignore the implication that time moves faster through this rift. That would be..." Galloway fished for the proper word, "...unscientific."

His greedy heart beat faster.

At his age, there would be no more chances to prove himself. It was desperation alone that caused the Company to seek him out and he refused to miss the call.

Five men were press-ganged into joining Doctor Galloway's expedition. Sharma and Bhatt packed the camels as the black growth shifted and pulsed.

In Hindi, Jacob asked the men if the mass always moved this way. The unfortunate lascars exchanged a look. One answered.

"Before, it moved like treacle. Now it is faster."

"It is a creature ready to give birth," the other man added, then averted his eyes to the pack. "We will die today, Doctor."

As they drove the camels closer, a noise grew.

The ambient slurp remained, but now it gnashed too, like a cyclone devouring debris.

The hum beneath their feet became a rumble and from the gash, nightmare beasts spewed forth by the thousands.

Galloway's chest thumped from the reverberations, as though his heart threatened to flee its cavity. His head rattled in accompaniment, teeth clacking together.

Black feet and talons trampled the men to death in bloody ribbons.

Yellow eyes flared as legions of hellspawn surged forward.

The shambling, screaming figures made no sense; every terrible monster twisted together in one throng.

Animal shrieks shredded the air, accompanied by human ones. Sands wet with blood released a metallic stench into the air.

Galloway vomited and collapsed, as bloody talons advanced on him. The impact knocked his watch to the ground, case open. It had wound down, but there would be no chance to wind it ever again.

A scaly creature with coarse fur and great claws sniffed him with a cat-like nose, then dove in and disemboweled him in seconds.

Galloway screamed and choked on the remnants of his vomit.

As he lay, death both immediate and eternal, the blackness leaked in a slow wave until it swallowed the tents and then moved on, perhaps to the rest of the world.

Whatever the Company ripped from the beyond, the end times were upon them now.

The last thing Jacob Galloway saw as he was dragged into the void was a rope of his entrails in the demon's mouth and piles of corpses in the sand.

Poetry Break
By Sarah E. Blackburn

TOXIC MASCULINITY

What did he do to his wonderful boy?
He let him down and stole his joy.
Gave him a rap upside the head,
When he needed to cry, was told to "man up"
instead.
Stifled, what an amazing man he could be...
Toxic Masculinity
Such a pestilential stream of consciousness,
that created this mess.
Passed down generation to generation
The idea of Domination.
Suppression, Aggression and the Ultimate Depression.

OCEAN DEPTHS

I stand looking out at the ocean
Its depths, the depths of my everything
The clouds are electric, against the silver backdrop
Seagulls swishing and sailing through the crisp air
My father's soul inhabited one, or maybe all, of those graceful sky dancers.
For once, all that's unresolved dissipates
And now I feel forgiveness for the first time in this existence.

Tears fall for the close stranger, who never let me know him.
And I let go of the thoughts that anything could have gone differently.
I feel a deeper love for what I couldn't always see, to appreciate.

Fever Dream

Do you feel the heat of the summer days, baby?

Do you feel the cold winter nights, baby?

Could you let me love you all the ways, baby?

Grace muted the radio on her dashboard so hard the screen rattled. She pulled her car into her reserved parking space—*apartment 133 only!*—and turned the engine off with too much force. The keys came sliding out and dropped to the floor under her foot.

"Fuck it. I don't fucking care," she said to herself. The headache she had this afternoon was long gone but the fatigue was worse in its place. *For a while, it'll always be one or the other till your body adjusts,* Doctor Cross told her.

Grace buried her face into her palms. It smudged her makeup, making little spider trails under her eyes that would soon resemble a raccoon. But it didn't matter if she removed the mascara, her eyes would still be black underneath. That was another effect of the transplant, but Doctor Cross and company said it would go away, too.

"Once my body adjusts," she said into her hands. She sniffed.

The car made cool-down clicking sounds and she listened to the rhythm of it, like rain on a tent in the middle of the woods. She longed to go back to the woods for a long week or two of solitude. Maybe soon.

But not when she had to be right near the hospital for emergencies. Like the out-of-control fever she had the week before where she called for services seconds before she fainted, only to wake up in a tub of what felt like freezing water. The concerned faces of three nurses and one doctor standing over her, the doctor telling her to stop shivering.

"You put me in an ice bath, of course I'm going to shiver," Grace looked at Doctor Cross with wide eyes and a scowl.

"It only feels icy—it's actually lukewarm," the doctor said. "Please, try to keep still."

So she did, and now she was in her car, after another day at work monitoring the temperatures of chill storage and filling out paperwork. She was in her car with her hands to her face, wondering why in the fuck she bothered with the transplant in the first place.

"For all this? A studio apartment, a dead-end job, and a— well

I guess the car is okay," she said. "But what's the point in the rest of it? And who am I talking to?"

Grace picked her phone up from its holder on the dash and flicked it on with her thumb. No messages. Nothing.

Since the transplant, the people who called themselves 'friends' had been conspicuous in their absence.

Friday nights that once consisted of dinner and drinks at Taco Tate's Mexican-Irish fusion restaurant (enjoy our Guadalupe Car Bomb!) and a ton of laughter and bad jokes now consisted of a platter of microwave egg rolls and sleeping on the couch with a film playing as background noise.

Maybe I should get a pet.

Grace took a deep breath. "No, fuck this feeling sorry for myself bullshit." She took her hands away from her eyes and looked in the rearview mirror, then chuckled. Time to suck it up, take a shower, change her clothes, and call someone to ask them out.

She grabbed her purse from the passenger side floor, then looked up.

That's when she spotted a woman. A deformed woman.

Oh, it wasn't kind to think of someone as deformed, Grace corrected herself. *A woman with deformities, god damn it—not like you're perfect, Gracie.* The woman looked like someone squeezed a tube of toothpaste from both ends and broke open the middle. Short of something physically oozing out of the person standing near the hedges, the comparison was apt.

Grace looked down for a moment and pulled her sunglasses out of her purse, then put them on. The reflective mirrors allowed her to espy the woman in more detail without outright staring.

But that was what this woman was doing. She was staring at Grace so hard the weight of her gaze seemed tangible. Grace squirmed internally. She hated when people looked at her too long in the first place, and this woman was extra creepy—and not because she had withered limbs and an awkward-squeezed-tube body. No, most cases Grace would just note it and move along, because *don't be rude to people who are different.* This was something more.

The woman was dirty, as though she hadn't washed in a month, with her greasy, short hair corkscrewed on one side and an enormous cowlick on the other.

She had a slack-jawed stare that showed teeth that were dark brown and large gaps in between. Her blue sweatshirt had a film of brown on it and her matching sweatpants did no better. One leg was all the way down to her ankle and the other was rolled up to her knee.

But perhaps the biggest thing that put a lump in Grace's throat and made her heart do triples was the fact that the woman seemed familiar.

She couldn't place her–and wouldn't her features stand out to her? Maybe she'd seen the woman at the homeless shelter where she'd volunteered a few years ago.

Grace dawdled as long as she could, pretending to root through her purse to find something. The woman gaped at her the entire time.

After a few more minutes of gathering her things (and being bored into by two dull eyes), she picked up her keys from the floor and laced them through her fingers. Just in case.

Dialing emergency services and hovering her one hand over the 'send' button, Grace made a coordinated effort to emerge from the car in a manner true to her name. She closed the door with her hip and made her way onto the sidewalk, looking away from the woman, but eying her from behind her mirrored shades. Her hands gripped the keys as she neared the other–in order to get into her apartment, she'd have to get close. Likely within grabbing distance. Grace braced herself for the inevitable panhandling or cultist literature–or whatever this woman wanted.

Grace's heart beat harder and a sense of anger washed over her–of self-righteous anger. *I have the right to walk on my own goddamn sidewalk to my own goddamn apartment.*

The long, confident strides didn't falter as she rounded the small corner that led to the breezeway.

"He's inside you now," Homeless Woman said.

"Okay," Grace said, then mentally kicked herself for even acknowledging the words spoken to her. *Move on. Keep walking.*

As she attempted to get past Homeless Woman, her legs moved with a swiftness Grace didn't expect, and she pulled back, preparing to raise her fist.

"My father is inside of you," Homeless Woman held up a hand that only had one large finger on the bone, and a thumb. It was as if the bones were fused. She pointed that finger up towards Grace's neck.

"He's inside you."

"Well he should've taken me out to dinner, first," Grace said. "Go away."

"No. This is everyone's sidewalk. I have a right to be here."

Grace sidestepped and made another attempt to move forward, but the woman got in front of her again.

She marveled at just how fast she could move on such tiny legs.

"Then get out of my way and enjoy all the sidewalk you want," Grace made a growling sound in the back of her throat.

The woman wasn't willing to relent. She pointed again to Grace's neck. "There's my father. He's stuck in you for good."

In an instant, it clicked.
Her neck–the transplant.

But how would this woman know about an experimental CNS fiber transplant?

It saved Grace from becoming a quadriplegic and made her a frequent visitor of the emergency room as of late (Doctor Cross knew her by name, as did most of the staff), but this was nothing that Homeless Woman could know.

Sure, it was in the news, but Grace never gave permission to be revealed to the public and the doctors discussed her case in vague terms so the public didn't even know the recipient's gender.

Even her friends and colleagues didn't know all the details. Some friends knew the truth, but never blabbed. They didn't come around anymore, but they weren't the type of people to run their mouths, either.

"Ah, so you think your father lives on in me—well, I won't stand here and argue–I think your father should be thanked for making such a generous donation of his organs and tissues, and that's all I can say on the subject."

Grace looked down into the woman's dull eyes that were some kind of dark gray with flecks of brown in them. In the low light of the dying day, they looked black.

"Good day," Grace said, and stepped forward again.

The woman held up both hands, and Grace saw that her opposite hand had three fingers. The two on the hand had that fused look in some kind of eternal 'V' gesture, and the thumb looked too big, too swollen to belong on there. She tried her best not to stare, instead looking back into the woman's eyes.

"No, it's a bad day. My father lives inside of you now."

Homeless Woman looked like she was either going to cry or attack, and Grace prepared for either. She wasn't keen on hitting a woman with so many issues, but she'd defend herself if it came down to that.

"Yes, well, in a way he does, but really, your father is dead. I'm sorry for your loss and grateful for my gain."

"You won't be grateful, not if you knew what was inside you and growing," the woman circled one finger in a small motion, as if pinpointing the area where the nerve fibers were donated. Which was insane because the fibers were all over her spine, really.

"I need to go now," Grace said, trying again to walk past the woman—now named Donor's Daughter in her head. "I'm visiting a friend who needs me."

Donor's Daughter sidestepped again on those matchstick legs. "No. No. You live here. Don't lie."

Grace, tired from her long day of temperature controls and filling out maintenance requests, eager to get home and maybe visit with someone who didn't forget about her, snapped. "Get out of my fucking way, you disgusting fucking gimp!"

For just a moment, Donor's Daughter looked up at Grace as if she'd been hit with a bucket of cold water. But her round 'o' of a mouth turned into a smile-snarl that showed almost as much gum as tooth. Grace could see a bubble of mucus coming out of the woman's nose and her stomach flipped itself inside out.

Yet Grace was more surprised with what came out of her own mouth than what came out of the woman's nostril. She put her hand to her lips. She'd never called anyone a 'gimp' before, and that kind of cruelty was foreign to her. Her face felt too hot and her eyes stung with tears. She was glad for the sunglasses.

"You see?" Donor's Daughter said, "you're already starting to change, aren't you? Yes—it's happening."

The woman took a step to the other side and shuffled away. "He's there, inside you," she said as she walked off. "He used to call me that. It's him. I know it. You'll be sorry. Too late, too late."

Grace's hands shook as she adjusted her keys to open her apartment door and hurry inside. Her legs felt weak and watery and a film of sweat broke out on her face. Her whole body felt like she'd been in a fight, and for a moment, the entryway seemed there and not there. A dizziness washed over her and she leaned back against the door, sliding down it until her bottom hit the floor.

Reaching behind herself, one long arm ending in a strong hand locked the lowest deadbolt behind her. She crumpled, bringing her hand to her forehead. "It's okay. It's over. She's gone."

She remembered what it was like when she first woke up from surgery. They told her she wouldn't be allowed to lift her arms or legs, but she couldn't have, even if she'd wanted. They'd felt like dead weight—so much so that she first thought the staff had put her in restraints.

That was how she'd felt when she came inside. The restraints were on and she needed to get to the floor before she didn't have a choice. Once the adrenaline died out a little, Grace found her strength to stand again.

Her hands stopped shaking and she put her keys up on the hook, then dropped her purse in the catch-all basket by the door. She put her phone in her pocket and made an immediate left to enter her kitchen.

The apartment's kitchen was the showpiece of the apartment. Since she liked cooking, it had been ideal for her at the time she moved in two years ago. A year later, she stopped cooking anything. Her interest dwindled. She was weak and tired all the time. There were some days she couldn't lift her arms to shower.

Exhausted, she went to a doctor.
He said she was depressed.
He wrote her a scrip for antidepressants.
Didn't draw blood, didn't do much of an exam, either.

Five days later, she couldn't talk.

She pissed herself. She lost her sense of smell. Danielle had been with her—an overnight guest. She took her to the emergency room. Doctor Kathryn Cross told her she had a disorder called Esther-Kuipers Syndrome.

"Esther who?" Her friend asked Cross.

Given that Grace could only nod and shake her head, and write on her tablet, she was letting Danielle speak for her.

"Esther-Kuipers Syndrome," the doctor pulled up the rolling stool and sat with them, putting her tablet at the foot of the bed. "EKS, for short. It's a genetic disease that wears away microscopic holes in your CNS. Eventually the fibers weaken, and whatever they're connected to stops working. Unlike ALS, which is a sclerosis from scarring of the disease, this one eats away and dissolves the connections. Eventually, it will cause you to stop breathing without a machine to assist. It's terminal. I'm sorry."

Grace felt tears slide down her face and realized she could barely control that anymore, either. Her body had become a prison.

Only death would free her.

Doctor Cross looked from Danielle to Grace, and her focus stayed on Grace.

"I have to be honest with you. It's a grim prognosis, and there's typically no chance for recovery. Eventually the microscopic holes will eat through a nerve you need to breathe, or keep your heart beating, etcetera."

"That's awful. There's nothing we can do?" Danielle asked.

Her eyes were so wide Grace thought it looked like she'd taken mescaline.

"Normally, no. In all cases, EKS is fatal—but there's something new that we can try."

Grace managed to nod and invited the doctor to tell her more. She scribbled a question mark onto her note app with the stylus she held. *Please go on.*

"Have you read anything about Doctor Vo Pham?" Doctor Cross looked back and forth between the other two women again, and when they both shook their heads, she continued.

'He's a surgeon—a transplant expert on the CNS—central nervous system, and he and a team of neurosurgeons have been working on a project here in Grace City. The Center for Health Assurance has approved their proposal for human trials."

Danielle frowned, but Grace sat forward and wrote on her app. *What human trials?*

"For a transplant of human nerve fibers and stem cells that would regrow your nervous system. Much as it did when you were an infant, but on a full-grown scale. I'd best leave the detailed explanation to him. But based on your profile and that you were in good general health before this started, Ms. Foerster, and the nature of your condition, I think you'd be a good candidate for the Pham Trials. It's high-risk—I can't stress that enough—and you'd be the first, so we can't even give you success rates or what the outcomes will be, but I can assure you that there is no other treatment at this time, aside from palliative measures."

So I'm going to die for sure, then? Grace wrote out and showed it to the doctor.

Cross nodded. "Just like the rest of us, but given the rapid deterioration of your condition, I don't think you will be with us much longer. I don't like to give estimates but given how fast your system is degrading, you need to decide as soon as possible."

Estimate, Grace wrote.

"If the disease continues to progress at this rate, you have about a week, maybe two. Now, I can give one day to make your decision but the transplant window is closing. It has to be before the degradation is too severe so the CNS can be retrained."

I don't need time to decide. I'm taking a chance. Give me the paperwork, whatever, Grace wrote and showed Doctor Cross.

"I'll call the team and get them here, and have them get you the consent forms. Do you have any family I should call?" She gave Danielle a nod, as if to ask if they were a couple. Danielle shook her head.

"Her parents are deceased and she has a brother, but they're estranged. We wouldn't know where to find him," she looked over at Grace, who shrugged, then wrote on her tablet. *He's probably dead.*

Grace nodded at the doctor and motioned her closer. Cross leaned in and she showed the doctor what she'd written. *I have an advance directive on record here at the hospital. Don't know if you saw it.*

Cross nodded. "I did. If you want to update it, now's the time."

Grace shook her head. *If I die, I die.*

After she left, Grace filled out the paperwork and made Danielle go home. Though she was reluctant, she left. She woke up surrounded by Doctor Pham and three neurosurgeons, and with all the efficiency of a Helvetic clock, she was made whole again.

Until today, she didn't regret any of it.

Aside from a few lifestyle adjustments and some setbacks, plus some funny dreams, Grace had spent the last year being stunned by the fact she was still alive. She was alive to have bad days like this one. The dreams, though.

Dreams of fucking. Of having a big strap-on and thrusting it into any hole she could find. Sometimes the women were strangers. Sometimes friends. The newfound libido and interest in porn? A lust for life. Right? Happy to be alive, she wanted to feel everything. Some of her friends said she'd changed—the ones that bothered to stick around. Even Danielle gave her more space than before, but Danielle was a flight attendant. She was gone a lot. Then again, she hadn't spoken to Grace in six months. Not even so much as a text.

"Women are cunts," Grace said, then laughed. Sweat formed on her brow. No. She couldn't afford another fever. Fuck's sake, she just got home from another out-of-control one.

She had to lie down quickly, with aspirin and cold water. She chewed up an adult aspirin, washed it down with a glass of water, chewed up gum, and grabbed her ice packs.

Time to lie down.

She closed her eyes. The whispers, coaxing her into a fever dream, began. The darkness surrounded her and she swallowed. It felt like glass. The whispers grew, and Grace focused on them. Wherever she was, it was dark, and warm. A sliver of light to her right gave her enough illumination that she could see past the shadows. But the space was a void, only a shape in the center came to focus.

Danielle. She was curled up, naked. Whimpering.

"Why? Why are you doing this?"

Grace squinted and tried to see through the dark. Another form came into the graying light. A vague form of a man with elongated limbs and hooded. She couldn't see his face—there was a full facial covering, even netting over the eyes. He didn't speak.

He reached into a pocket and pulled out something green. A bottle.

Danielle cried for him to stop. "Please, what did I do wrong, why was this happening?"

The tall man didn't answer. He took the bottle and shoved it inside her. Her words climbed to incoherent screams. He thrust the bottle into her, deeper and deeper. She didn't try to fight anymore. In fact, she hadn't tried to fight in the first place—she just screamed, then gave up.

He's weakened her, Grace thought.

Danielle was a fighter. This had to be a dream. She could make out dried blood on her behind and thighs. This wasn't his first attack on her. Grace moved in, holding her breath, and saw more than the blood. Her muscles were wasting away and her skin hanged from her bones. She'd been here a long time.

He laughed as she rolled away from him, struggling to sit up, to move. "Weak. You disgusting little fuck. Dry bones are all that's left of you."

A whisper-whimper escaped Danielle's lips. He finished with the bottle and stood up. "What did you say?"

"Why are you doing this?"

He answered by smashing the feces-encrusted bottle over her head. Jagged glass remained, and he laughed again. The man bent down and grabbed Grace's friend by her hair, pulling her face upward to meet his.

"Because it's what you deserve. It's what you all deserve," he said. Jagged glass pierced the softened, pliable skin on her forehead, and the man traced the bottle down around her cheeks, her jawline, and stopped at her chin.

She screamed and tried to pull away from him, backing herself against a wall. He moved with her, still cutting deep, until the skin loosened and fell onto her chest. It reminded her of a bloody sheet mask.

Grace woke up, stomach churning, but she could tell her fever was gone. All that was left was dried sweat. She looked down at herself. Blood on the sheets.

Blood on her knuckles. Grace sighed. She'd managed to thrash around in her sleep yet again, as evidenced by the bits of skin on the side of her bed table. The image of Danielle's skin in her own lap sprang back to mind. Grace leapt up and barely made it to the toilet to dry heave.

A half-gallon of water later, she felt like herself again. That was another thing they'd warned her about since the transplant. She had to stay extra hydrated—to stave off her immune system from launching antibodies. That's what caused a lot of the high fevers.

She picked up her phone and sent Danielle a text. *Hey, sorry I've been distant. Things are weird lately. When you're home, can we have a visit?*

There was no answer for a half-hour. Grace took a shower.

As she was smoothing lotion over her always-ashy knees, her phone buzzed.

Sorry dude u have the wrong number

You're not Danielle? She sent back.

A picture popped up of a dick.

Unless Danielle's got one of these, no. Fuck off scammer

Grace's heart hammered in her chest as a thread of rage bubbled up inside her—what the fuck? She blocked the number and sat there, hugging herself. It wouldn't do to get another fever by stressing about this.

More important, though—where was Danielle? Did she get ghosted?

Last time she saw her was six months ago, and Danielle was about to do the Oceania-Australasia route. They didn't end on a happy note—Dani had told her that she'd changed a lot. So much so she didn't really know if they'd continue their friendship.

Guess that was her answer.

But that still didn't sit well with Grace. It still didn't. She opened her friend's profile page. Maybe they were still friends there and she could send her a message.

There were messages all over Danielle's wall. Messages of "missing you," and "where could you be?"

And finally, a pleading message from Danielle's mother.

Please, if anyone has seen Dani or has any information, contact your local police or the Center for Missing and Exploited People. We just want her home safe and sound.

"Oh," Grace said. "Well, that—was a little after she visited me."

She shrugged. The police definitely would have questioned her about it. But they never did. It was like she vanished sometime between going home and when she was supposed to board her flight.

She clicked on the link for the Center of Missing and Exploited People and then clicked "send message." Maybe she could help the cops trace their steps.

The red badge in her messenger distracted her. A little red 1. Someone cared, at least. Or maybe it was just spam. Looked like spam, but Grace clicked on it anyway. The sender was named "Disabled Account." Grace rolled her eyes. It wasn't even clever.

The message was a picture. A picture with a caption: *this you?*

It looked like her, but the location didn't look familiar. Some kind of amusement park. Was there an amusement park around here? She shook her head. The photo looked recent, but the last time Grace had been to amusements was when she was sixteen years old. With her first crush—a girl named Suzy.

Suzy had been painfully beautiful and so zaftig—nice and cushioned with lots of softness. Grace smiled to herself—a lecherous smile as the thoughts of looking her up and maybe playing with her for a while flowed through her.

Her attention wavered back to the Disabled Account picture. This was recent, though. Maybe a couple of months ago—it was before she got her new haircut and wore it up-styled.

She clicked on the name of the account.

This account has been disabled.

Grace frowned.

There were no pictures left on it and nothing that told her who this was. Could it be one of those AI thingies? The ones that paste your face onto another person? She supposed that could be and that's why the account had been deactivated. Maybe that was a scammer thing.

She shrugged. Grace had to get up and run errands anyway. Maybe she'd track down Suzy, ask her on a date. The reason Suzy had left in the first place was because she liked sex better than Grace had, but with this newfound sexual desire—well, maybe they'd be compatible again.

Grace left to go on her errands. She'd find Suzy later. The day was beautiful and the store wasn't far, so Grace took her handcart and walked the two blocks to the store. It was one full block before she realized she was being followed.

Donor's Daughter.

Weird. She wasn't sure what to do. The woman was clearly bonkers, following her around. But maybe she wasn't following her. Maybe she was just homeless and missed her medication or something.

Grace used to volunteer at the soup kitchen all the time but now she was always too busy, either dealing with her own fevers and anti-rejection meds, or engrossed in porn that was new to her. Torture porn, for example. Watching fake snuff films. Sometimes she just watched and laughed at how fake they were, but other times...

She couldn't let her mind wander like that in public. Just the thought of excitement was enough to make her blush. Grace looked in a shop window, checking both her own reflection and that of Donor's Daughter across the street. DD must have caught on—she turned and hobbled in the opposite direction.

For a moment, Grace thought about turning around and following her instead.

See how she would like it. She smiled at the thought of following her, harassing her, yelling and tossing things at her. She laughed at the absurdity of picking on and bullying a cripple, then felt guilty for even thinking something that mean.

She took a deep breath. That fever had really gotten to her. Maybe she'd mention it to her doctor next appointment.

Groceries got, Grace wheeled her little hand-cart home. It wasn't till she approached her door that her smile faded.

A wall of printed photos plastered all over her front door—not the kind that came from the drugstore kiosk—but professionally developed ones. She ran to the door with her cart behind her.

Pulling the photos down, she dragged them and her cart inside. She could guess who left the photos on her door, but how did DD move so fast? She knew she shouldn't think those bad things about people—but this was ridiculous. She didn't deserve to be harassed.

Especially by a useless cripple.

"Stop that," she said to herself. She looked through the photographs. They were of her, out places. Places she'd never been. She couldn't have been. She hadn't been well enough to do extensive traveling as her body changed and adapted to her new implant.

She put the photos outside, tossing them into her storage shed.

When she came back inside, she called the police. "We'll send someone over to check on you," the man said.

After she unpacked her groceries and settled down to her ramen and frozen veg, there was a knock at her door. Grace jumped, then realized it was probably just a cop. She checked through the peephole.

A man in a police uniform. She opened the door a little and peeked out at him. "Just checking your badge," she said.

"Check away. I'm Officer Shitbag. You wanna tell me what happened?"

"Um—I'm sorry, what did you say your name was?"

"Shepherd. Are you Grace Starling?"

"Sterling," she said, trying not to sound annoyed.

"Yeah, right, Sterling. May I come in? I just need to take your report."

She hesitated, then opened the door wider. "I was just eating dinner. You know, since it took so long for you to get here."

Officer Shitbag (her misheard name was more fitting) scoffed and helped himself inside, taking a look around as she ushered him to the dining area. Grace sat back down and motioned for him to take a seat, too. He whipped out a digital notepad and stylus, then sat down with her.

"Okay, whenever you're ready."

"I'm being harassed by a homeless woman—she came to the door yesterday, I think it was yesterday."

"You 'think' it was yesterday?"

"Yes, I've been sleeping from a fever, so it could have been the day before. I have a hard time keeping track of the day when I come out of a fever."

"You're sick?" Shitbag inched away from her.

"No—not contagious, anyway. I'm a transplant recipient. But that's not really important. Call it yesterday, a homeless lady came over and started harassing me."

"About what?"

Grace felt her throat tighten. She shook her head.

"Nothing that made any sense," she squeaked out.

"Okay, what's her name? You got a description, a picture, what?"

"She's kind of deformed. About my height, but she looks like a halfway squeezed tube of toothpaste and her hair is dirty. I can't tell the natural color because there's a lot of dirt in it. Her eyes were a kind of hazel brown, and she was really filthy."

"Yeah—doesn't sound familiar. You got a name on her? Address?" Shitbag wasn't writing anything down. Grace took a bite of ramen and sighed.

"No. I don't recall her name if she said it, and I assume she doesn't have an address. She's probably at the local shelter. Alastor's Oath."

"And what's she doing? Is she threatening you?"

"Yes. She grabbed me—and she keeps coming by the house, and following me to the store. I just want her to leave me alone. Can I get a restraining order?"

"For what? She grabbed you. But come on, Miss Sterling, she's a cripple. You can stop her."
Shitbag stood up.

Grace scowled. "I can't really stop her from harassing me if you don't tell her to stop."

Shitbag shrugged. "We can't issue a restraining order on a crippled homeless woman—she needs to have a name and we need a place to go to find her. For now—we'll track her down and if she bothers you again, call us."

"That's it?"

"Yeah, well, not much more to be done, really. I promise, we'll keep a lookout for her and tell her to leave you alone." Grace stood up and headed for the door. "That's so super helpful," she said. "I mean, you really made me feel better about the whole thing."

Shitbag raised his eyebrow at her, but didn't say anything in return. She locked the door behind him and bolted it shut.

"Fuck stick," she said. Her head was starting to hurt, and now she was starting to sweat.

Grace took her medicine and sat back on her recliner. The fever took over, and so did her descent into dreams. Dreaming of finding Suzy, running her hands up her skirt, and finding twisted limbs. She looks again, and it's DD, but Grace didn't stop, even through DD's protests.

DD screamed for help. "Please—what are you doing?"

Grace laughed. "Nothing you don't remember, nothing you don't want."

She woke up with a gasp, surrounded by monitors, and an alarm going off. Grace tried to sit up, but a nurse with a tight-cropped haircut rushed into the room and pushed her back down with gentle but firm hands.

"Don't sit up too suddenly."

Grace resisted—why was she in the hospital? Why wasn't she still in her living room? She waited for the nurse to let go of her and help her sit up.
Her limbs felt heavy.
Trembling.

The nurse brought her a cup of orange juice.

"What happened?" Grace asked.

"The police brought you in," the nurse said. "What day is it?"

"Uh—I'm not sure, actually. Last thing I remember it was August 9th."

"Today's the twelfth," the nurse said. "You've been here since last night. Do you remember anything?"

She shook her head at the nurse. "What happened?"

"You came in with a high-fever and delirious. We couldn't understand you. But we know you well enough around here—your case, I mean. I'll let the doctor fill you in on the details when she gets here, but girl you gave us a super scare this time."

Grace felt her head swim and the orange juice threatened to come up, but she swallowed it down.

"I don't like scaring the nurses in the ER—you know that's got to be bad."

"It was a high fever. You kept getting up and walking around all night, too. So we had to put you in restraints till you fell asleep proper. How do you feel?"

"Like I need to pee. Hungry, too," Grace said. "Thinking that's what's upsetting my stomach."

"Well, if you can get up, toilet's around the corner. Doctor Cross will be in to see you in a little while."

"But we're here to see her first," a man's voice said.

"Officer Shitbag," Grace said under her breath. "Uh, Shepherd," she amended with a raise of her voice. "What's wrong?"

A woman in a suit came in with him and Grace looked alarmed. Did she do something? Was Danielle dead?

"Well, you were pretty wrong when I came to see you," Shitbag said. "I came back with the detective to ask a few more questions. This is Detective Jennifer Ma."

Detective Ma gave Grace a wave.
"Glad to see you're awake. You feeling up to a few questions?"

Grace nodded. "I don't remember how I even got here, but yeah, I can try to answer questions."

"Well," Shitbag said, "I came back last night with Detective Ma and you didn't answer. I remembered you said you were a transplant patient so I thought I'd do a wellness check. Good thing I came in—you were burning up and screaming something. Sounded like a different language or something. Anyway, we brought you here and now you're better."

Grace shook her head. "I don't remember that at all."

"It's okay," the detective said. "I wanted to ask you about the lady that kept bothering you. I have a couple of photographs. If you can tell me if any of them fit her description I can help you with a restraining order. We just need to know who she is."

Grace gave the side-eye to Shitbag, then back to Ma. "They said there wasn't much they could do."

"Well, maybe not, but we can try," Ma said. "Have you seen her lately?"

Grace shrugged.

"Not since the store. After I reported her, I got sick again. My fever spiked. I wound up here. So I wouldn't know if she stopped by or anything."

Ma put out a few pictures. "Here are some of the women who fit your description. We don't have body pictures but all of them have some visible disability. Can you tell me by their faces which one?"

Grace shook her head.
"None of these women. Her face was more angled. I'm sorry."

"No, don't be sorry," Detective Ma said. "We'll check out the shelters, see if she pops up."

Grace nodded, shoulders slumping. "Thanks."

"If she bothers you again, here—take my card," Detective Ma handed it to her. "You call the number on the back. That's my mobile. Okay? You call anytime."

Grace took the card and held it in both hands.

"Thank you. I will."

Shitbag shrugged and left with Ma trailing behind him.

"You think we'd get a 'thanks' for saving her life," Grace heard him say.

"Fuck you," she said, but he was well out of earshot.

After breakfast, Doctor Cross came in to see her. Grace brightened—Cross was really attractive. No hope for them, though. She was also strictly professional.

By the time she was discharged with a new prescription and a referral back to her treatment team, it was dark.

She took a cab home and scurried into the apartment, feeling like she was being watched. She took her new medicine, waited for the side effects, and fell into a blissful sleep.
No dreams.
No fever.

When she woke up the next morning, she found a note stuffed under her door.

Where have you been? The note read.

No photographs.

Grace threw open the door and looked outside. She spotted DD in the bushes by the edge of the breezeway.

"Nice to know you're thinking of me," she shouted.

DD moved towards the door. "I have to tell you something. You have to listen to me. Maybe it's not too late. There's still a chance for you."

Grace moved back to slam the door, but a feeling—a gut reaction—told her to wait. She did. "I'm going inside to cook some breakfast. You hungry?"

"I could eat," DD said. "You're—you're inviting me in?"

"Yeah," Grace said. "Look—I'm not evil or a bitch or whatever. I've just been through a lot. Looks to me like you have, too. So why don't we sit down and talk? It can't hurt, right?"

Grace opened the door wide and motioned for her to come in. DD hesitated at first, then headed in. "You can sit at the bar while I cook. Eggs and toast. Sound good?"

"Ah, that sounds nice," DD wriggled her way onto the barstool, using her arms to stabilize herself.

Grace watched her, then realized she was staring.

"Sorry, that's rude of me."

"It's okay—I'm used to it."

Not knowing what to say to that, Grace made the coffee and started breakfast.

"We got on a really bad start," Grace said as she set the table. "I'm Grace Sterling. What about you?"

"Deenie Wall," she said. She moved over to the table and sat down. Grace ignored the smell of Deenie's stint on the streets by favoring the fresh poured coffee.

"Deenie, that's funny—I'd been calling you 'DD' in my head," she said.

"Oh? Why? Disabled Diva?" Deenie said. "Dirty Deed?"

Grace looked up with a mouth round with shock but then laughed when she saw Deenie was teasing.

"Donor's Daughter—I would say Dirty Diva has a burlesque sound to it though."

They ate breakfast. Deenie focused on the food and coffee, not saying much until she was finished. Grace poured out more coffee.

"A heavy silence fell between them," Deenie said. She looked up at Grace. "That's what I'd write right now if I were describing what was going on."

"Well, let's clear it up," Grace said. "Tell me what you wanted to say before I shut you down and told you to fuck off."

"I suppose I could've been better about telling you—but I was scared," Deenie said. "It's—it was like looking into my dad's eyes. Looking into them and seeing the darkness."

Grace suppressed a shiver. "So—he wasn't a great guy, huh?"

Deenie shook her head. "No. He was—it's hard to talk about it."

"You don't have to—you can just give me the highlight reel if you want," Grace said.

That seemed to startle Deenie. "The highlight reel, yeah. Well—my father didn't want me. Used to tell me that all the time. But he liked to play games with me, even when I was a baby. I don't remember that. Games where he'd see how much he could get away with."

Grace swallowed her coffee, trying to keep a poker face as she listened.

"He was an attorney. Super respected in our community. Everyone said my mom was a 'wild woman,' you know? She ran off when I was two. I don't remember anything about her except for a floral print dress with blood on it. My father told me she didn't want to have a baby. What I didn't know was that he burned my birth certificate and told everyone she'd taken me with her."

Grace's eyes widened. "Are you for real?"

"For real. We had a panic room in the house. That was my room, sealed off from everyone and everything. I had a bed, a toilet, and a bath. And every night, for sixteen years, he would come in and play games with me. He would break my bones and leave them broken. He experimented with my muscles, seeing if they'd grow back. He fused my fingers together."

Grace felt her breakfast settle in rock form. "That's—evil."

"You don't believe it. There are too many questions," she said. "Why didn't anyone check on me? How was he able to set me free? To keep me alive?" She shrugged. "Like I said: he was smart, he was cruel, and one day he knocked me out so hard I woke up sixty miles out of my hometown. I came here. No skills, no jobs. I was eighteen with no birth certificate and only the name Deenie Walls, which isn't his name. It was my mother's."

"I don't want to know his name," Grace said. "I don't want that kind of—kind of—sickness inside me."

"I figured maybe if I warned you, maybe you could stop it. Be aware of what's growing inside of you."

Grace poured out two more cups of coffee and pulled her mug closer as if to hug it. "I was dying."

"I know."

"I mean, what good is it telling me, though?"
Deenie shrugged. "If you get weird urges, maybe you can stop them."

Grace sighed and sipped her coffee. "So how did you find me, really?"

"You don't remember me but we met a lot at the soup kitchen. I never introduced myself. Just took my meal and bread.

Always thought you were so pretty—but I got shy. Sometimes I can't even speak when I get shy. It was a long time before I could actually even tell anyone my name. I never spoke to people. Just paid my quarter, got my bread, and slept at the shelter. Then you stopped volunteering. You got busy, I guess before you got sick. I wondered where you were. I wondered what happened to my father."

Deenie shook her head.

"I know this sounds stupid, but I had an instinct—something was wrong with him and I just knew it. So I decided to track him down. I played a long game of connect the dots—and using the computers at the library, I posed as an old friend from the Bar Association and found him."

Grace felt her heart beat harder. She didn't say anything—she didn't want to say anything.

"Found out he was at the hospital and decided to pay him a visit. I told them I was his estranged daughter, gave a pretty lie to the charge nurses there, and they let me see him."

Grace found her voice. "What did he do?"

Deenie shook her head. "He was out of it—his surgery hadn't gone well. He was on his last legs. But I wasn't about to let him wake up. I cut off his oxygen, and with a little luck, he went into something called V-Fib. He flat-lined and died. They couldn't revive him, though I let them try."

"I don't blame you," Grace said. "Seems like you let him off easy."

"I didn't want him to recover. They said he was suffering—so maybe I did him a favor, but I wanted him gone. I didn't know he was an organ donor until they had me sign for his belongings. Then—well—then I learned that they were using his CNS for an experimental transplant. I didn't really think about it until..."

Grace leaned forward. "Until what?"

"Until I managed to track you down. I got scared—I thought he might try to come back."

Grace laughed. "Your fears are unwarranted. I mean, I probably love porn a little more than I used to, but I also love life and appreciate the second chance I'm getting. I'm not going to be your dad."

Deenie shook her head. "I'm sorry. I just remember the old superstition, and since it was a whole CNS transplant, I thought maybe he lived in you in a bad way."

"Maybe I just got the best parts," Grace said. She smiled and patted Deenie's hand. "I'm still the same sweetheart who used to serve food over hot trays. I can't do it anymore though, not until the transplant is finally settled and stops making me sick."

"Sick?"

"Yeah. My body is still trying to adjust and adapt to the foreign body inside of it, but eventually it will—or so they keep telling me—and once it does, it'll be a full part of me."

Deenie took a sip of her coffee. She wiped her mouth on her sleeve. "I hope you win."

"Me too. But I'm sure I will."

Deenie gave her a wide-eyed look. "I better go. I've bothered you enough."

"It's not a bother. In fact, why don't you use my shower and we go through some of my clothes, put yours in the laundry? You can stay a while, sleep on my couch. I know it's not much, but it beats the cots, right?" Grace gave her hand a quick squeeze. "I insist."

"No—I don't want to put you out," Deenie said. "Especially after the way I acted."

Grace laughed.

"Shush. We'll consider it a misunderstanding. Stay. I absolutely insist."

After a shower, choosing some of Grace's cast-offs, and a nap on the couch, Grace made lunch for them both.

"I really can't impose," Deenie said.

Grace shook her head. "I'm not holding you hostage. I mean, if you insist on leaving, go ahead, but at least take the lunch with you. And you can always come back if you need anything."

She walked Deenie to the door, lunch packed and a thermos of hot coffee in hand. Grace locked up once she was gone, then turned to face her kitchen.

There was blood on the counter. Blood, and a little bit of hair.

Grace reached up and touched her forehead. She drew her hand away to see a mass of blood, some skin, and her own hair in her palm. A pit of unease made her stomach quake, and she threw up in the sink.

Deenie's plotting something, Grace thought as she fell to the floor. Had she already fainted and hit her head? Was that why the counter was bloody? She's plotting your demise, you dumb bitch, a voice in her head said. You can't let her.

Grace woke up in her bathtub, water running and lukewarm. Another fever had taken over, and she thanked herself for having the smarts to climb into the tub in her delirium. It probably saved her yet again.

Now how much time had passed? She found her phone in the bedroom as she toweled off. Three days had passed.

Three days. She had managed, through her fever, to clean her kitchen, lie in bed (the pillow had some blood on it too), and then bring herself to the bathtub to lie in cool water until the fever broke.

Grace checked her phone. No messages. She tried not to think about it—wondering if she really had become that unpleasant to be around—so much so that not one person in her circle of friends had ever come by to see how she was doing. She supposed it was possible. It still stung.

As she was dressed, the tub drained and freshly bleached, and her head wound looking healed (she was even able to cover it with a beanie), there was a knock at the door.

"Detective Ma," Grace said, she smiled. The detective didn't smile back. "What's wrong?"

"Is this the woman that's been bothering you?" Detective Ma held up a picture of Deenie.

"She was. I mean, I've been sick again, laid up for a few days, so if she was bothering me I wouldn't notice."

Ma tapped the photo. "She's missing. Someone at the soup kitchen reported her gone."

Grace shrugged. "I mean, she's indigent—maybe she wandered off."

"Maybe—but she's a regular apparently. You sure you haven't seen her?"

Grace shook her head. "No. I've been bedridden. This is the first day I haven't had a fever in half a week. I mean, how long has she been missing?"

"They think about four days."

"She's plotting something," Grace said.

Detective Ma cocked her head. "What makes you think that?"

"She—she came by before I got sick. She started telling me things about her dad, her abuse, her past. I thought she might be making it up. She left, but I don't know. I felt weird about it. I tried to be friendly to her thinking maybe she'd leave me alone. She said she killed her dad. Maybe I'm next."

"Did she threaten you?"

"I mean—she hinted at how easy it was to kill her dad, and I don't even know if that's true or if she made it up."

Ma sighed. "She could be making it up, who knows? But don't engage her if you see her again. Call us instead, okay? It's probably nothing, but we need to be careful. You need to do whatever you gotta do to ensure you're safe. Okay?"

"Yeah," Grace said. "I will. I'll call you if she turns up again."

Detective Ma left and Grace shut the door. She laughed, and didn't know why.

The fever returned that night, and Grace saw a pile of bodies in the dark space, where Danielle had once been. But this time, it was a pile of limbs, disjointed, falling off their bones, skin sagging and mummified in some spots, maggot eaten and rotting in others.

Deenie was on the top of the pile. Splayed. Grace watched through someone else's eyes.

"Daddy—stay away! Help! Grace? Help me, can you see me? Grace?"

Grace was outside the body at that moment, watching them, helpless as the hooded figure stabbed Deenie through her sternum. No blood. None until Deenie coughed and it came out of her mouth. The man laughed, took a brick, and bashed it into her skull.

Grace screamed for him to stop, and woke up as she did. She was sweating. Chilled. She shivered and gasped heaps of air. The bedroom fan was off.

"I need air," she whispered in the dark.

The apartment patios were large enough for a porch swing, barbecue grill, and a small table for two. She made her way to the swing and sat. The cool night air brought a gentle breeze with it, and her skin, so hot to the touch, cooled enough that she was comfortable.

A smell, rotten and clinging, wafted to her nose. A skunk? No. A dead skunk? Maybe.

She sniffed, turning her head to the direction of the smell. It was emanating from her storage shed. Grace opened the gate and crossed the narrow path that led to the shed adjacent to her flat. That was another blessing of this place —the sheds big enough to store a car. But the neighbors would start complaining if she had any dead animals trapped in there. Best to deal with it and carry on, even during another threat of fever.

She could call the maintenance manager in the morning, have him help her clean it out. They were nice to her since her operation, at least.

A tickle in the back of her neck teased its way up her scalp and she shivered. The fever was getting high again.

She opened the door, shutting it behind her. Light switch flipped. Nothing.

Grace sighed and felt around her pockets till she found her phone. She flipped on the flashlight and looked ahead so as not to trip on anything.

A leg. A human leg. Decaying.

The leg, on top of a torso, on top of a pile of arms, on top of breasts. Pieces of people. Pieces of women.

Heads. Danielle, Patience, Marcy, Jennie, Jewels. Every single one of her friends, heads neatly arranged at the bottom of the pile. Grace held back a scream, cramping seized her throat. She fell to her knees on top of a bisected torso and wailed.

She screamed, body seizing, lying down in the pile until she gagged out peals of laughter, sinking into herself. "So much work to do, you sloppy girl."

Her hands trailed down to the inside of her pants and she laughed, rolling and frolicking in the decay. As she tittered and cried out, The Donor stepped forward. "Get up, Grace. You've so much to do."

The fever broke.

ONE WEEK LATER

Grace, feeling more alive than she'd ever felt before, woke up late and went out to collect her mail. She grinned to herself and sang a little song.

Do you feel the heat of the summer days, baby?

Do you feel the cold winter nights, baby?

Could you let me love you all the ways, baby?

Will you let me inside forever, baby?

Ballad interrupted by the presence of her two least favorite people at her door, Grace plastered on a smile and greeted them. "Officer Shepherd. Detective Ma. What brings you here?"

"This," Ma said. "This is a search warrant."

"I know what it is—I went to law school. But just two of you? Where's your team?" She snatched it out of Ma's hand and read it.

"They'll be here—but you could make it a lot easier if you give us what we're looking for."

Grace shook her head. "No. You're going to have to look. I won't deny that Miss Wall was here on the date this warrant says, but she left, and she didn't leave anything behind."

"Right," Detective Ma said.

An hour later, Grace stood on her patio, smoking a cigarette. The doctor didn't like that she'd picked up the habit, but not even death could stop him from his favorite vices.

Smoking, fucking, and cutting up whores. The fun-holy trinity.

"What's in the shed?" Detective Ma asked as she came out onto the porch. Grace set her jaw, then smiled. Oh, wouldn't she love to add that head to her private collection?

It wasn't meant to be. Grace gave her a pleasant smile.

"That shed? Tools for the barbecue, and rat traps."

"Mind if I take a look?" Ma said.

"Yes, I mind, and no, you may not look."

"There's a funny smell in there. I can smell it all the way out here," Shitbag said.

"Dead rats, and a raccoon got into the walls. I have to get in there and clean it out."

"Well, we need to take a look."

Grace laughed. "Then you should have gotten 'all adjacent structures' added to your warrant, Officer Shitbag—I mean Shepherd."

Grinning, Grace shooed them off the patio. "Go away. I don't have what you want and you know it. You've made a mess in here that I've got to get cleaned up."

Grace almost added that she had a date tonight—but that would be tipping them off too well. Her grin turned to a smirk as she showed them out the door.

She heard Shitbag talking to Ma. "Hey. I don't remember she ever went to law school. Is that in her file?"

Whistling as she closed and locked the door, Grace packed a bag, took her cash, and drove until it was time to ditch the car.

Walking down the highway, she stuck her thumb out at the first car passing by. A couple of young women. Grace gave them her friendliest smile.

Two more for the collection.

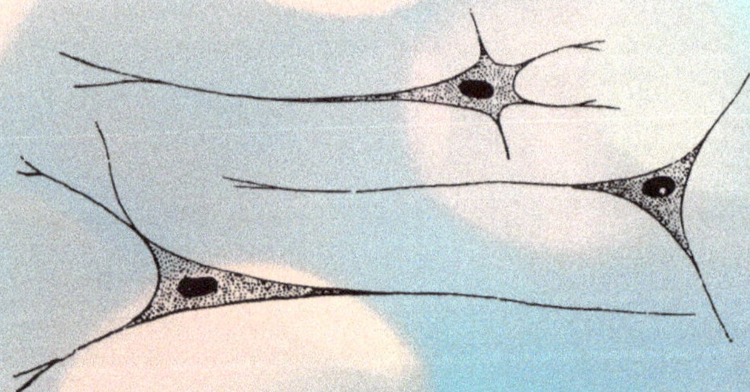

END CREDITS

Lucienne LeBeau would like to thank the entire team for being incredibly supportive and bringing their evil energy A-game. We could not have done this without your sublime contributions. Special thanks to W.P. Quigley for giving this project wings. Great appreciation to all our staff and much love to our contributors. I am surrounded by talent and overwhelmed by the sheer energy donated

Nix Black, Art Director - thank you for making this issue beautiful, I cannot wait to see the final results of your vision. For this and more issues to come.

Michael Strong - thank you for your wonderful cover and taking us back in time to the sewn seeds of toxic masculinity. I could not appreciate you more.

Sarah E. Blackburn - thank you for your beautiful poetry and for making even more to come. You paint a picture with your words.

S. N. Humphreys - thank you for an entertaining and a 'heap' of a story where the witches win. We all needed that story whether we realized it or not.

D. S. Vernon - One of the most talented copy editors and proofers I've ever met. Thank you for your enthusiasm and dedication to quality product.